And They Came with Haste

ENDORSEMENTS

There is nothing like the satisfaction you discover when you finish reading a good book. The words paint a beautiful portrait on the canvas of your mind. The love of reading becomes a doorway taking you to places and ideas you have never encountered before. It brings such joy to the journey you are taking with each turn of a page and the start of another chapter.

Writing a book is not an easy task. It becomes more difficult to the author when a familiar phrase is used. At first glance of the title, the reader may automatically assume the direction this book is going to take. However, you will quickly be amazed at the creativity and twist of imagination in this unique work.

And They Came with Haste will cause you to read with haste as you are drawn in deeper with each word, line, paragraph, and chapter. Then comes the ending like a grand finale. You will be astonished!

One other word of warning. Don't be surprised if you find yourself wanting to get additional copies to share with others.

—Dr. Calvin Ray Evans, Rubyville Community Church, Pastor; Evangelistic Outreach Ministries, Director

Whitney Ward uses the gift of imagery and description to teleport her readers to a Bethlehem hillside, observing the life of a Jewish girl who faces the pull between tradition and longing. Every young reader will easily identify with the wistfulness and hope that comes with finding God's calling on their life. Hadassah possesses a love for her father's flock in a culture that expects her to love tradition more than anything else. Join Whitney as she leads you along this inspiring journey as Hadassah discovers that God uses unexpected circumstances to lead our lives toward the unbelievable outcome.

—The Christmas Cave, Presented by White Gravel Mines

Orphan, bummer, or cull—they go by many names. All of them point to two things—lots of extra care needed and a short life span. Seldom do they reach full maturity, and most remain smaller and weaker than the others. Yet, in these weak, fragile, and vulnerable creatures, we caretakers find the greatest gifts. Their reflective lives show us both what is base and best in ourselves. I invite you to discover the gifts Hadassah and Haste share with each other and the world in this moving story from my young writing friend, Whitney Ward.

—J.D. Wininger, Award-Winning Writer and Speaker, Rancher and Owner of Cross-Dubya Ranch in Texas

And They Came with Haste

Whitney Lane Ward

A Christian Company
ElkLakePublishingInc.com

COPYRIGHT NOTICE

And They Came with Haste

Cover and Interior Design: Derinda Babcock, Deb Haggerty
Editor(s): Cristel Phelps, Deb Haggerty
Author Represented By: Cyle Young Literary Elite

PUBLISHED BY: Elk Lake Publishing, Inc., 35 Dogwood Drive, Plymouth, MA 02360, 2022

Library Cataloging Data

Names: Ward, Whitney Lane (Whitney Lane Ward)

And They Came with Haste / Whitney Lane Ward

162 p. 23cm × 15cm (9in × 6 in.)

ISBN-13: 978-1-64949-740-6 (paperback) | 978-1-64949-741-3 (trade hardcover) | 978-1-64949-742-0 (trade paperback) | 978-1-64949-743-7 (e-book)

Key Words: Jewish tradition; Jewish women's roles in Jesus's time; shepherds; betrothal and marriage in Jewish tradition; Nativity; Special Gifts; Biblical Fiction

Library of Congress Control Number: 2022947552

DEDICATION

To my sweet friend and prayer warrior, Lola. When you were my teacher at Vacation Bible School, we instantly connected, and over the years that bond has grown MORE precious. You have been one of my biggest cheerleaders and encouragers. Your strength has made a profound impact on my life, and I just want to tell you thank you. As I always say, I want to be you when I grow up! Love you!

ACKNOWLEDGMENTS

To My Parents

Mom and Dad, even though I was the one fighting my chronic illness, I know it still profoundly affected you too. When parents watch their child experience pain in their body and face frightening uncertainties due to illness, it breaks those parents' hearts in the worse possible way, and they wish they could take their child's place. While your heart ached for what I endured, you always put on a brave face for my sake, encouraging me to never allow my disease to control me, but to look for precious moments that would allow me to live life to the fullest. You supported my desire to surpass my limitations, even when those limitations seemed impossible to overcome. Above all, you taught me to trust God because he had a purpose for my life despite my disease. Your belief and confidence in me gave me the courage to face the unknowns surrounding me. The selfless love, dedication, and devotion you poured into me has had a profound impact on my life and has helped shape me into the woman I am today. I thank God he gave me the parents he knew I needed, who were the first people who showed me that I am MORE!

To My Sister

Linsay, Mom and Dad always laughed and said God knew which daughter could handle pain and medical procedures. While God gave me a high pain tolerance and the ability to not dwell on the "what if's" and unknowns, you were given the gift of compassion and a selfless heart—the sister my soul needed in the midst of my heartache and confusion. Growing up, you were always there when I was sick, nursing me back to health and making sure I had what I needed. That stability in my ever-changing world was like a soothing and healing balm to my invisible wounds. You always told me I could achieve my dreams even if they seemed unobtainable to others, and you were my protector and stood up to anyone who would dare to tear me down. You aren't just my sister; you're my best friend!

To My Grandma

How I adore my silly, fun-loving, selfless Grandma! Your house was a haven for me. My life revolved around doctor's appointments and having no energy to do anything but lay on the couch, but I could come to your house to get a change of scenery that lifted my spirits. You allowed me to pour my heart out to you about the pain and weight I carried from the treatment I received from other kids—your listening ear and validation of my feelings lessened the burdens I felt and helped me keep climbing. The fact you accompanied Mom and me to almost every doctor's appointment while I was growing up meant the world to me—it took my mind off any procedures or tests I was dreading, and I treasured the extra time I got to spend with you. Thank you for always going above and beyond to show me I matter!

To Those Who Have Gone On

Oh, Grandpa, how I miss you! I miss our early morning garden adventures of picking corn, green beans, and tomatoes. I miss your lessons on putting out a proper garden and learning your tricks to produce a successful harvest. I miss your famous PB&J sandwiches and your ability to fix anything. You were a one-of-a-kind grandpa with a heart of gold! I will forever be grateful you accepted Jesus Christ as your Savior two weeks before you passed away, and I have the peace of knowing I will see you again!

Memaw, I can't believe it's been seventeen years since you went home to be with Jesus. Although miles separated us, I couldn't wait every summer to visit you in Georgia, and the year you came to spend Christmas with our family in Ohio will always be a precious memory to me. I only wish we would have had more time together, but I'm so glad we will have eternity to spend together catching up!

Grandad, I was just two when you passed away, but I'm so glad you accepted Jesus as your Savior before you passed away, as well, because I'm so excited to get to know you!

Papaw Trim, Mamaw Marie, Papaw Alvis and Mamaw Marg, not many people have the rare opportunity to know their great-grandparents, but I did. Thank you for the rich heritage you left in my life!

To Those Who Have Helped Me

Enormous gratitude goes to my assistant pastor, Brian Baer. I can't tell you how much it meant for you to trust me to write *And They Came with Haste*. What you did not know when you asked, I was going through a very dark time in my life, so this writing project came exactly when I needed it. This story gave me a purpose, allowed me to get lost in Hadassah and Haste's world, forgetting my own struggles, and helped me see some light during the darkness. Thank you for giving me this gift!

I would like to thank my agent, Del Duduit, who has walked me through the publishing process, answering all my questions and calming all my worry. I'd also would like to send my profound appreciation to Deb Haggerty for believing in me and making my dream of becoming a published author come true. And lastly, I would like to acknowledge my editors Megan Jacobs, Cristel Phelps, and Deb Haggerty—thank you for working hard to make my book all I hoped it would be!

FOREWORD

Christmas is my favorite time of the year. As the years have passed, the reasons have changed. The kid in me ALWAYS enjoys opening gifts! However, the more mature me enjoys the time with family and reflecting over the birth of my Savior.

One day, I was listening to Luke chapter 2 from a Bible app on my phone. As the narrator came to the words, "And they came with haste," he paused. Immediately, my imagination focused on a disabled little lamb being carried by a shepherd. Perhaps it was the recent viewing of the television classic, *Rudolph, the Red-Nosed Reindeer*, or the personal struggle with my own self esteem which led to these thoughts. Regardless, if the former or latter, I could not shake the vision of this little disabled lamb.

Did he realize he was intended to be a sacrificial lamb? Was he aware, due to his disability, he would never meet the qualifications of a lamb without blemish? I began to feel sympathetic to his situation knowing he would never live up to what was expected of him. Regardless of his condition, he was not thrown away. He would become the pet of the shepherds and ultimately meet the last Lamb to be offered for the sins of the world.

The destination of these nomads was to see the Lamb of God born in a manger. From that moment, each time

I reread Luke's account, I could not help but think of "Haste." This fictional character remained in my mind for many years. I mentioned the idea to Whitney Ward. My intention was to create a children's Christmas play and eventually, showcase the drama. I simply had no time to author the project and asked her to take full rein.

I am so glad I let go! Whitney's adaptation of this idea is far more than I could have dreamed. This fictional account has now been brought to life. The inspiration in these pages may perhaps help a struggling child to keep pressing forward. God cares and loves EVERYONE, regardless of stature, age, or race. May we all find encouragement in these words and realize no matter our station, we can come with "Haste" to meet the Savior of the world!

—Brian Baer

Honorary Doctor of Divinity, Assistant Pastor of Rubyville Community Church, Assistant Director of Evangelistic Outreach

A word glossary is provided in the back of the book to explain the lesser-known Jewish words and traditions used in *And They Came with Haste*

CHAPTER 1

For several generations, my family raised sheep in Bethlehem.

That is all I have ever known. From generation to generation, the flock passed down from father to oldest son. And since Papa was the oldest of his family, he inherited the flock.

The sheep were used for many purposes—wool for clothing, milk for nutrition ... and the most important purpose? Sacrifice—to atone for Israel's sin. Each year, Papa would make the trek from Bethlehem to Jerusalem to sell to the priest the male lambs fit for sacrifice. And they were fit—"only the best for God," Papa liked to say.

Bethlehem's endless and prosperous rolling hills and babbling streams made raising sheep the trade for many men. Custom said the youngest son was to be the shepherd of the flock until, eventually, every son would receive the honor of being the family shepherd. When the patriarch became wrinkled and gray with age, the oldest son inherited the flock—his birthright and blessing.

Other men had sons. Papa had daughters.

This honorable tradition between father and son caused Mama to apologize with each child she bore. "Samuel, my love, I am sorry it is not a son." She spat in exhaustion. She held her newborn to her chest with fierce protection, unaware she almost dared Papa to be disappointed with the daughter she'd produced. Papa would smile and softly caress Mama's damp and salty forehead. "I care not if it is a son or daughter. I care if the child is healthy. Besides, Rachel, my daughters will be more than worthy wives. Not only will they know how to run a household, but they will also know how to run a flock."

And that is exactly how my parents raised my four sisters and me. The daughter who was the family shepherd would rise at sunup with Papa to attend to the sheep. After the midday meal, she remained home with Mama to learn the makings of a proper Jewish home and honoring Yahweh when managing a family. In the afternoon, our two hirelings assisted Papa, and then, the hirelings would sleep with the flock at night.

Our neighbors marveled at our family. A daughter's place was in the home at the knee of her mother. But Papa and Mama determined our house would not function on legalistic ideologies but would be filled with love and compassion. The women in Papa's household were not just objects to be used for cooking, cleaning, and child-bearing. All of us had a purpose and a contribution to give.

As the youngest shepherd of the family, I remained with the flock the longest—until I was betrothed at the age of thirteen. Yahweh gave me a special love for and fierce protection of my flock, and I determined to give them the best.

My sisters were always eager to remain home and work with Mama. Disappointment's hand clutched my heart when my time with the flock ended.

But Papa insisted I learn how to become a proper wife. I craved adventure. I wanted my purpose to be bigger than being some man's wife. I understood the importance to be taught the ways of the household because I knew a marriage union was my fate as it is for every Jewish woman. My head knew this fact, but at the end of each day, my heart was with the flock.

The sheep pasture was my place of peace. With the gentle winds causing the wildflowers to wave at me, and the sheep grazing in the luscious green grass, my world felt perfect. The slow days were my favorite. I would play the flute our hireling, Andrew, carved for me. My fingers perfectly touched the five melody-producing holes. I pretended it was a harp and I, Hadassah, was a master musician like King David. The sheep gamboled about in delight, and I knew I was the center of their whole world.

The first time I defended them terrified me. Once, when I was eight years old, the sheep became restless, not leaving my side. A lioness crouched on a rock near a mountain, waiting for the opportune time to come after her prey.

"Papa!" His teaching became my instinct, and I stiffened my limbs as a statue. "Look up on that rock—there is a lioness!"

Papa's stance mirrored my own, and he followed my gaze to the beast. His sun-kissed finger pointed. "Hadassah, the time has come for you to defend your flock."

His words almost caused me to run, which would only signal the lioness to pounce. "B-but I cannot! What if I fail them?"

Papa did not falter in his confidence. "I have taught you what you need to know. Your flock trusts you, and with that trust, combined with the help from the LORD your God, you will not fail them."

My hand trembled so much as I grasped, with difficulty, one of the stones I kept in my receptacle. The lioness saw my movement and responded with a deafening, vicious roar. She jumped off the rock, running swift and smooth as wind. The predator's intent hid nothing. I placed the small smooth stone in my sling, and righteous indignation fired into my heart. No lamb would leave my flock today.

I swung the weapon several times around my head, then, taking a large step forward for leverage, I launched the stone with all my might. Papa and I watched as the stone sailed in the air, hitting the lioness's back with amazing accuracy. The blue sky echoed with howls of anger and pain.

The sheep recognized the victory. They leaped in joy about my feet, their happy bleating blotting out the lioness's defeated whines. An exhilarating warmth filled my cheeks. My calling was complete and sure. I had kept my sheep safe, and God had provided my first victory. I knew the Lord placed the mantle in my hands to be this flock's protector.

But just as Papa taught me how to protect and care for the sheep, he taught me to learn from them as well. I turned six years old the day I became the new shepherdess. It was on this day that Papa gave me wisdom I will remember until the day I go back to dust. He placed his hands on my small and delicate shoulders, our eyes leveled. Already feeling the importance of my role, I took Papa's words and hid them in my heart. "Hadassah, just as Jehovah Jireh has a purpose for every person, so he does with every lamb. And on a rare occasion there might be a lamb that has a divine purpose."

I did not really understand his words. My pure innocence told me my sheep's purposes were to be my friends. Years later, I understood how true Papa's words were. You may assume Papa's prophetic proclamation rang true in a strong, perfect lamb, fit for sacrifice—but it was quite the opposite. The divine purpose came in a maimed lamb ... a lamb I named Haste.

CHAPTER 2

"Hadassah ... Hadassah, it is time ..."

I slowly opened my eyes as a voice in my dreams woke me up from a slumber I did not want to leave. My dreams sometimes took me on an unexpected journey a young Jewish girl could only ever long to experience. Some nights, I stood on the bow of a ship as a merchant, sailing for Greece to deliver priceless goods. Other nights, I sat in the temple among the young Jewish boys learning the Law and receiving an education to become something other than a wife and child-bearer.

I closed my eyes and rolled over with a sigh. *What could it be time to do?*

"Hadassah ... Come, my child."

My eyes opened in surprise at the very real and urgent whisper. Heat filled my cheeks as my eyes caught the dark silhouette the sun cast on the thin curtain hiding my sister and my quarters. I sat up slowly and rubbed my face, willing the blush to disappear.

"Coming, Papa." I assured him.

I changed into a fresh tunic and braided my black curly hair—or at least what I could of it—my thick unruly locks could challenge a bed of thistles, and pain came with trying to untangle it. Glancing at the still body of my older sister, Lydia, I shook my head. I envied the adventures her dreams still took her on, but I would not change the reason I rise with the sun each morning. As the youngest daughter, I had a special role. A role I felt Yahweh called me to.

I was the family shepherd.

I walked into the main living area of the small cabin. Sometimes, I cannot fathom how Papa and Mama managed to make our home feel so big while raising five daughters. I believe the feeling came from the love and respect Papa and Mama gave each other and their children. God and the family had been the order of our dedication.

"We need to hurry. Jonathan and Andrew probably have their hands full with baby lambs that came during the night." Papa's hands moved quickly as he put bread and cheese into his receptacle.

I yawned and slipped my coat over my tunic. "I am sorry. I love my flock, but I had a difficult time rising this morning."

Papa stroked his grey beard and chuckled. "What morning do you *not* have trouble rising, my daughter? Were you dreaming again?"

The familiar heat hugged my cheeks once again, but I managed to smile. "Yes, Papa, I did have a dream. I do not remember what happened, but the realness of it made me believe your gentle prodding to arise was a part of my dream. I found myself looking at Lydia and envying the dreams and rest she still experiences."

"I am not surprised you dreamt last night since it is a special day for you."

My black eyes became as round as the coal they resembled. "My birthday! How did I forget I am now eleven?"

Papa smiled. "I do not know. You must be getting forgetful in old age."

I grinned and rolled my eyes. "Yes, that must be it. I will have to trade my shepherd's staff for an old hag's cane."

Papa winked. "Well, my child, in two years' time, you will have a long slumber."

My heart quickly dropped, exposing the fear it held, just as the walls surrounding Jericho quickly crumbled exposing the city within. "Papa, that is not what I want to hear. Especially on my birthday."

Papa stared at me and then dropped his eyes, saying nothing, because he had already lamented his belief many times. A daughter of Samuel and Rachel's would have the ability to tend to a flock as well as learn the skills and knowledge to run a Jewish household. I knew Papa did not intend to be cruel—it caused him great pain to see the fear in my face because of my inevitable and foreseeable betrothal he would have to arrange in a year. The intimacy a husband and wife shared filled my sisters' souls with excitement and curiosity ... this mystery crushed my soul with dread. I understood a marriage for a woman was not only Jewish custom, but protection from certain vulnerabilities. But I have come to learn, understanding and acceptance of a situation does not so easily shift the longing of one's heart. A truth Papa and Mama did not fully see.

"Let us be on our way, Hadassah," Papa told me, his eyes not meeting mine.

We grabbed our staffs and left our home. The peaceful silence, the birds chirping, and the pink streaks highlighting the dim sky, signaling the beginning of a new day, contrasted with the tension between Papa and me. I hated this. Papa and I shared a close and unique bond. It crushed my soul when he did not seem to understand my feelings. But I refused to apologize when I did nothing wrong. The balm to our hurting hearts came into view.

The sheep immediately flocked to my side and danced in delight at my feet. Joy leapt within my heart and freed itself by my laughter. Kneeling down, I petted the soft wool of each sheep and looked up to find Papa smiling at me, our disagreement forgotten. Smiling back, I turned my attention back to the sheep with a thankful prayer to Yahweh that our flock could be a bridge for us.

The size of the the flock showed the wealth of a man, and with a flock of only thirty sheep, clearly, Papa did not hold much wealth to his name. I would not want it any other way. This flock provided for our family, and because of its small size, Papa could manage it with two hirelings and me. A blissful world of our very own. Papa and I loved this flock and would not trade it for any other way of life.

"Samuel, Hadassah! How are you this morning?" Jonathan, one of our hirelings, greeted.

"We are well!" Papa told Jonathan and our other hireling, Andrew, giving them both a firm handshake.

"It looks like we have some new lambs."

"You are correct, my lady. One of the ewes has not begun the lambing process yet, but the other two ewes that were pregnant gave birth in the wee hours of the morning. There are two new males and two new females."

"Are they healthy?"

Andrew grinned. "Quite. Both ewes had normal births, no complications. The little lambs are nursing well, and the male lambs are without blemish. I expect they'll take their first steps soon."

"Good! The male lambs will make excellent sacrifices next year. Good work, Jonathan and Andrew. Now go home and get some rest. I'll see you this afternoon." Papa assured them.

"Oh, one more thing," Jonathan added. "We allowed the flock to frolic, and we had to pick off barbs and thistles from several of the sheep's wool. They will need oil."

The two men walked until they became distant dots, blending in with the landscape. I turned to look at the pregnant ewe, who should have given birth already. Being a naturally petite ewe, she had been larger with each stage of her pregnancy. Normal for any small ewe expecting a lamb. But today, a prickling instinct told me to watch and be ready.

"Papa?"

"Yes, Daughter?"

"I'm concerned about the ewe that has not given birth yet."

Papa leaned on his staff."Why, Hadassah?"

"She seems rather late and hasn't even begun the birthing process yet."

"Some go past the time they should give birth."

I shook my head, wishing he could sense the urgency rising within me. "I know. But something does not feel right."

Papa did not answer right away, but his hand stroked his beard as it does when he is deep in thought, and he examined the animal. I knew he believed my thoughts had merit. I do not know why, but Elohim engrained in the fibers of my being a keen understanding of my sheep.

When the flock faced danger, I could sense it. When a lamb battled sickness and needed soothing, I knew exactly how to minister to its ailment. And when one of the lambs became sad, l knew what to do to lift its spirit.

Rough callouses scratched my shoulder, causing relief to fill every pore of my body. "I trust you, my girl. If you feel this way, we'll watch the ewe closely."

"Thank you, Papa."

"Now let's get to work. There is much to be done."

Perspiration's invisible hands slid down my face tickling my cheeks. I wiped the salty water with my arm, thankful for the March winds keeping Papa and me cool as we worked. *Swoosh ... swoosh ... swoosh ...*

The milk echoed hitting the clay pitcher. I pushed the ewe's teat up and squeezed it with gentle ease, trying to get every ounce of milk she could provide.

I set the pitcher aside and withdrew the bottle of oil I kept in my receptacle. I grabbed the wool under the ewe's chin and looked her in the eyes. "Listen, I know you despise when I pour this oil down your head, but just know I do it for your own good." I tightened my grip on the sheep's wool and poured the thick oil onto her head. The ewe yanked her head back and forth. She bleated in frustration.

I held tight as I watched the oil stream down her head into her eyes and nostrils, essential to prevent parasites making their home in the sheep's nose.

"There you go, girl." I patted the ewe. "I'm through."

I stood up and wiped my oily hands on my coat. I watched as the sheep I just anointed trotted away, rubbed her head in the grass to remove the excess oil, and then looked at me in defiance. I chuckled as I picked up the pitcher and placed it with the other four that were filled to the brim with milk. The flock would never understand many of the things we do as shepherds were for their own good, even if they seem unpleasant at the time. Papa often liked to compare our job as shepherds to our covenant with Yahweh. Many times, God allowed things to happen to our people that we did not like or understand, but God, as our shepherd, knew it was for our own good.

CHAPTER 3

I put my hands on my hips and leaned back to stretch my screaming muscles. The hours kneeling to tend to the milking caused every body part to ache. I loved it though. The sky glistened and shimmered like the ocean on a clear day. The position of the sun and the rumbling of my stomach told me what I needed to know. I had two hours before the noonday meal. No time to rest. I began the grueling task of grooming each sheep. Sifting through every inch of wool, I removed any tick or flea present on the animal's skin. Leaning on all fours, I checked for sores and cuts on their limbs. Two rams had cuts on the backs of their legs. I reached into my receptacle, pulled out a small jar of ointment, and took hold of one of the ram's hind legs. "Steady, boy." I soothed as the ram swung its head back and forth. "Let me put this ointment on your leg, and you can go back to grazing."

I rubbed the ointment on the cut and then gave him a pat on the back, "There you go, all finished." His wet nose nuzzled my cheek in thanks, and he went on his way.

I sat down and sighed, my bones weary from the blood and sweat of the day, but the satisfaction of everything accomplished filled my soul. I looked at my flock in the green pasture of my father's land. They had not a worry in this world. Everything seemed perfect in the little world of the rolling hills of Bethlehem.

Almost perfect.

The baby lambs took their first steps, and the flock grazed happily because the rains had been plentiful. Life in this world should be tranquil, yet a cloud floated closer to overshadow the sun.

The pregnant ewe.

When would she begin lambing? She had all of the signs birthing was nigh—swollen with milk, ready to nurse her young, hollow hips, and a decreased exterior. When would the other phases of lambing break through?

Papa walked over and sat down. "I finished counting the flock. They are all accounted for." When I did not answer, he followed my black eyes to their subject. "Are you still worried about the ewe?" he asked using his sundra to wipe the drops of sweat from his face.

I released all of the breath I had been holding. A shepherd's emotions should not control them. The flock depended on its leader to be confident and self-assured. "Is my worry so much that you see it? I hope the flock doesn't sense it."

Papa pulled a strand of my hair and chuckled. "I'm not faulting you, Hadassah. You love your flock very much, and your gentle touch with them is as soothing as a doting mother. But I know you, so I can see the worry, no matter how much you try to hide it. However, I assure you, the flock is very unaware."

I picked a wildflower, twirling it around in distraction. "Thank you, Papa. I do believe we are going to have complications with this birth." Tears formed puddles at the surface of my eyes. I struggled to keep them in their bottle, but my fear clasped its invisible hand around my neck, threatening to strangle me. I exhaled and decided to cast my burden upon my compassionate father, for I knew he cared. "I have been the shepherd of this flock for five years, but I have yet to experience the death of a lamb. I have yet to utter the words, *tetelestai,* signaling the end of one of my sheep." Shudders shook my body. I almost welcomed the burn the tears caused because it matched the turmoil of my heart. "I don't believe I ever could perform that task."

I finally could muster the courage to look at Papa. My steadfast rock. I could not bear to disappoint him. This man had been the shepherd of this flock for over forty years. He'd uttered the death proclamation, *tetelistai,* for a beloved lamb many times. The word meant, "It is finished." He knew the pain of which I spoke. But I knew if anyone understood my fear, the dread of what could occur, he did.

Putting his arm around me, Papa drew my head to his chest. "I know. And we will watch her closely. There is nothing we can do for her right now. We will assist her when we can, but right now we have to let nature take its course as Elohim intended."

His words were a soothing balm to my wounds. I clung to his strength, to his wisdom. God the Creator had my flock, this ewe in the palm of his hand. I needed to trust. "Yes, Papa."

Papa pointed to the four pitchers. "Why did you fill all of those up?"

"Mama wants to begin preparing for our journey to Jerusalem in a couple of weeks for Passover. I daresay she plans for us to make cheese this afternoon."

"She loves this time of year."

Breaking from his embrace, I gave his arm a shove. "So do you, Papa. Mama just lets it show more. But I have observed you. You watch all of us with a smile on your face, not knowing where to look because you do not want to miss one precious moment."

Papa let his head fall back and let out a rich laugh. "What you say is true, Daughter. I can't hide the pride I have for my family. It's not every day a man gets to be with his whole family at one time. Even if your sisters and their families must attend Passover festivities with their husbands' families, I count it a blessing they can, at least, travel with us. I also love remembering our people's exodus from Egypt and how Yahweh took care of our people hundreds of years ago."

"Oh, I could not agree more, Papa. I love it too. All the stories you've told me of what God has done for our nation stirs gratefulness within my heart. To know I'm a part of the chosen race and that I serve the God who can perform miracles gives me such peace."

Papa smiled at me, his tender-hearted daughter. "I share the same feeling. And this is Lydia's last Passover as a betrothed woman. Next year, she will be married."

The special moment deflated like bread dough when it is rising, and a sudden gust of wind hits it just right. I do not know why he brought up the subject I had told him I did not desire to discuss. Maybe he thought to talk of the betrothal of the sister I have a rare and unbreakable bond with would cause my heart to open to the subject of my own betrothal. It did not. I had to work through my feelings myself. Papa had an irrational need to make everything right in my world as his youngest child. We both knew this was impossible, but it did not stop him from trying.

"I am sorry, Hadassah. You expressed your wishes on this day, and I must respect them." The regret etched a triangle from his eyes to the tip of his forehead.

"Papa, you make me feel terrible. You know I love Matthew."

"I know."

"You have heard me speak praises of the care he will bestow on my sister."

"This is true."

"But the fact I approve of the union between Matthew and Lydia cannot erase how I feel."

Papa shook his head. "I do not completely understand your feelings, Hadasah, other than I know you do not want to leave your sheep, but the terror you have over marriage bewilders me."

I opened my mouth in defense, and Papa held up his hand. "Nevertheless, you have spoken what you need with grave respect, and I will not continue to push you. I am very sorry if I caused a rift to form between us."

I squeezed his hand. "That could never happen."

We sat in silence with our own thoughts when my eyes caught the very event I had been waiting for all day.

"Papa, look!"

He jumped in startlement, and I jumped to my feet.

We walked to the pregnant ewe. The white substance the ewe had just produced signaled the beginning of lambing.

"It is not much, Papa."

He knelt down and gently caressed the animal. "You are right. It looks like we might have a difficult lambing." I looked at Papa and saw he was finally worried about what might lie ahead. He began to stroke his salt and pepper beard. "But I pray to El Chuwl—the God who gives life—it will not be so."

Papa and I walked back to the cabin for the noonday meal.

"Do you think we should have remained with the ewe?"

"No, she is in good hands with Andrew and Jonathan. They know to watch her closely, and if they need us, they will get us."

I stayed silent. This was where my weakness lay. Not trusting Yahweh as I should. Whether it was with marriage or my beloved flock. I knew he had everything under control, but still the unknown frightened me. If God could protect my people from the evil Pharaoh with a pillar of cloud by day and a pillar of fire by night, he could keep this ewe safe. Only he could give me peace and acceptance on the intimacy of a husband and a wife must share. If he chose to. And this perhaps is where my fear stemmed from. Papa deeply believed in the words of Ecclesiastes. To everything there was a season, a time and place for everything. Which meant that if God chose it was this lamb's time to die, then there was nothing I could do. If God chose to allow my fear of a union to remain, then there must be a sovereign purpose. It surprised me to realize I was not angry at God. I took Father's teaching to heart that Yahweh had a purpose for everything even though I did not always understand God's ways.

We reached the cabin and used the pitcher outside to clean our hands and feet and placed our sandals by the door. As usual, Papa greeted Mama with a kiss on the cheek.

"The food looks very good, my love," he said surveying the bread, cheese, and almonds.

Mama beamed as if Papa gave her gold. "Thank you, my husband. Now let us eat."

I sat with my family around the low table that was worn with memories. We bowed our heads as Papa blessed the food.

"Yahweh-Yireh, thank you for providing this food, and please bless my wife and daughter for preparing this meal. We love you, amen."

We enjoyed the food Mama and Lydia prepared in silent contentment for a time.

"How was the flock today?" Mama asked Papa.

Papa's gaze shifted to me. "Do you want to answer, Hadassah?"

I nodded my head and looked at my mother and sister. "Overall, the flock is well. But we do have one pregnant ewe I am very concerned about."

"Why are you concerned, sister?" Lydia asked.

"She seemed very late in beginning the lambing process. Now that she has, there are indications it could be a complicated birth."

"But it could be a normal birth?" Mama the optimist inquired.

"Yes it could, of course, but still I feel we might have serious complications."

Lydia placed her hand over mine. As the last two daughters in Samuel and Rachel's household and with the closeness we shared, Lydia always knew what to say to put my heart at ease. "I have always admired your love for the flock. You have a connection with the sheep that neither I nor our other sisters ever had. Whatever happens, I know you will give your absolute best care to the ewe and her baby."

My heart contradicted itself—feeling peace and pain at the same time. I smiled. "I'm going to miss you."

"Well, you have me for another four weeks."

"I pray Yahweh slows down time as he did in the days of Joshua."

"Well, good." Lydia's voice was as dry as grain. "With as much cheese Mama plans to prepare, it may feel like time has stopped."

"Hadassah, will you go pick the apricots for the porridge?" Mama asked.

"Yes, Mama." I grabbed the small gathering basket, wishing I could have gone back to the sheep pasture with Papa.

I reached the apricot tree that was fully bloomed and ripe with fruit. I loved this time of year when everything burst forth in flourishing newness. I picked each piece of fruit deep in thought of my betrothal of all things. My family knew the apprehensiveness that clung to my heart because of my betrothal. They were as deeply rooted as an old fig tree. But what they did not know was the why. And the why reached deeper than any other root in the soil of my heart.

I was frightened I would not make a proper wife.

CHAPTER 4

Mama's teaching could not be faulted. I knew how to weave to make clothing, I knew how to cook, what foods not to serve together, and what foods were strictly forbidden for Jewish consumption. I knew all the logistics, all the rules, and all the traditions.

I could provide my husband with clothing for warmth, give him food for nourishment, but what of his other needs? What if I could not please him? I see the tenderness my Papa shows Mama. She is more than a child bearer to him, she is his priceless jewel. But as a Jewish man, Papa is a rarity. There was no guarantee the husband I would be given to would treat me like the woman spoken of in Proverbs 31. I could just be a thing for him to use. My cheeks began to resemble the color of the apricots. I could never voice these thoughts, not even to Lydia.

I picked the other apricots in quick order. I hated that my mind went to the subject I dreaded most. I had three years before any wifely duties began. Two years until my betrothal and three years until my marriage. When I become betrothed, I will be considered legally married. But thankfully, consummation would not take place until after the marriage ceremony—it was as if God gave me a personal act of kindness through this traditional Jewish law. I determined I would focus on what my heart loved.

My sheep.

"Andrew, Jonathan, I'm leaving for the night." Samuel spoke to the two hirelings.

"Very well, sir. We will take good care of the flock," Jonathan told his employer as he wiped the sweat off his brow.

"Thank you. Please pay close attention to the pregnant ewe. Hadassah is very worried there will be complications, and we know how much merit her intuition holds. It appears the lambing process has intensified, but she doesn't seem to be going through it as quickly as the other ewes."

"I will watch her closely, sir!" Andrew said before the older hireling could speak. "Uh, I—I mean we will watch her closely."

Jonathan smiled at him and winked. Samuel, however, did not notice the exchange between the younger men.

"I know I can trust you both!" Samuel slapped each man on the back in good humor. "See you in the morning."

Both men watched their employer walk away.

"Tell me." Jonathan grinned. "The fact that Hadassah is so worried about the ewe has nothing to do with you answering Samuel so quickly, right?"

Andrew's shoulders slumped forward. "Do my emotions show so much that everyone can see?

Jonathan chuckled and playfully nudged Andrew with his staff. "You forget, we spend more time with each other than anyone else—I see you more than I see my wife. Your endearment is discreet, but I see it."

Andrew shook his head and leaned on his staff. "I hope Samuel does not notice the love I have for his daughter before he begins to seek a husband for her next year. He will question my motives as his hireling."

"On the contrary, I think he would be pleased. He would be hard-pressed to find a better husband for his daughter."

"Thank you, my brother. It will be difficult to wait."

Jonathan smiled. "Patience my friend. Jacob had to work fourteen years for Rachel, and because of his love, those years seemed like mere days."

Andrew smiled, his posture showing his confidence had returned. "Two more years. Two more years and I can make my intentions known."

CHAPTER 5

"Another excellent meal." Papa leaned back and patted his stomach. "Is any other man more blessed than I?"

"No other man has me for a wife, so I doubt it." Mama did not smile, but the twinkle in her eye shone like the stars in the sky.

Papa chuckled low. "What you said is true, my love."

Mama, Lydia, and I began clearing our small wooden table. Lydia poured water that had been boiling over the fire into the washing bowl and each of us took an eating utensil to wash.

Mama studied the fine workmanship of the bowl she dried. "I just love these bowls and spoons. Samuel, please thank Andrew for me."

"My love, I have already thanked him three times for you. He knows they please you."

"He is such a talented carpenter. Why does he remain a hireling?"

"He sells his work in the marketplace, but he plans to remain a hireling until he gets married. Then he will set up a permanent booth in the marketplace." Papa shrugged, thinking his words settled the matter. He forgot he was talking to women.

"But why does he want to wait to marry?" Lydia asked while drying a bowl.

"He loves being with the sheep, but he also loves being a carpenter. While he is single, he can do both."

"But he has been with us for three years, Papa. I know there are many eligible Jewish women in Bethlehem."

Papa stared at Lydia and sighed. I did not have to ask what he was thinking because he had told us before—"I love my wife and daughters more than anything, but why do women ask so many questions? Especially when you have asked the same question over and over but changed the words, so it seems like it is a different question. No matter the way you ask it, the answer will remain the same."

A few seconds passed, and Papa rubbed his eyes. "Well, he is excellent help, so I can't complain."

"Maybe he is waiting for someone." My sister swung her cloth in with excitement. Poor Lydia. Because she was betrothed, she thought everyone's reason for living was to find their "someone."

"Yes." Mama agreed softly, her eyes focused on the spoon she had finished drying. "I believe he is waiting for someone too."

Papa rolled his eyes and waved to us. "Come, family, let us stop this nonsense. Please bring this absurd conversation and unfounded speculations to a close. It's time to read from the Law."

I rolled over to one side ... turned to lay on my back ... then once again I rolled back over my side.

"Are you asleep yet?" Lydia whispered.

"Yes." I elbowed her.

My sister used her elbow to prop up, the silvery shimmer glint of the night sky revealed her grin. "Commandment number eleven—thou shalt not lie."

"Hmmm, I do not believe that commandment is in my copy of the Torah." I wittily sparred back.

"That is because you do not have one."

"Well, you do not either."

Lydia and I looked at each other and giggled. Our light banter had always come easily.

"Well, Hadassah, I have something else I need to talk to you about, even though the eleventh commandment is a very good subject to speak of. I have wanted to speak to you since we ate the afternoon meal."

I stared up at the ceiling. "Somehow, I knew that."

"How many times have we had our talks under the moonlight?" This was Lydia's way. She told me she had something she wanted to talk to me about but then asked me a nostalgic question so I could prepare myself for what she had to say.

"I think I have lost count."

"I agree. Now we will have one more to count, my little sister. I must admit, it was very difficult waiting until now to talk with you. I knew that you would not want Papa and Mama to hear what I must ask."

I knew her words would grate on my heart. "What is it, sister?"

"Why did you get upset at the noon meal when you spoke of my leaving when I marry? I know you love the flock and thinking of my marriage only reminds you that one day you will be married and no longer the family shepherd. But you have never almost cried when speaking of it. There is more, is there not? Something you are not sharing with me?"

The familiar heat took root in my neck and grew to my cheeks. "I—I can ... cannot." Tears stung the corner of my eyes.

"Yes, you can. You can tell me anything."

My unwanted tears spilled down my cheeks, and I bowed my head in shame. "I am such a wretch for even thinking of such things. I am not even betrothed yet."

The softness of Lydia's hand touched my shoulder. "Hadassah, look at me. Come on, little sister. It is me who you are talking to. There is no need to be ashamed."

Unsure, I lifted my head, my black eyes looking into my sister's eyes that bore the resemblance of warm honey. I wondered if my eyes shadowed the yearning, the longing that she would understand.

"My heart breaks for you, sister. I think I know what you are alluding to, and I understand. Even though you are three years from marriage, you are still a girl. Close to marriage and yet still too young to be burdened with the ways between a married man and woman." Lydia caressed my cheek as if it was a priceless jewel, her eyes soft and tender. "I know even though you want to appear strong and capable, you desire to be honorable and please everyone. Even a man you will not know for another two years. Am I right?"

I took a deep breath and began to relax, because my sister was right. I had nothing to hide from her. Even when we did not agree, we still loved and admired each other. I just prayed to God she would accept my heart even if she did not understand it. "Yahweh has given us all talents. I am not blind to see that I am better with my flock than I am in the home with Mama. I long for more than being a wife. I want adventure and purpose. But I also fear I will not make a proper wife. What if I cannot make his favorite meal or mend his clothes as he prefers? Worse—what if I cannot give him children or I cannot s-satisfy his needs?" I rolled over to hide from my sister. The last admission made me feel vulnerable and exposed. I could not bear to look at my sister any longer, for the secret I shared contradicted every custom and tradition I had been taught.

I felt Lydia's arms wrap around me. "This is some of what I thought, Hadassah. First of all, you do better with the cooking and mending than you think. When the time comes, you will run your household with confidence. As for the other, I completely understand, I have had the same fears."

"You have?"

Lydia smiled, showing her dimples. "Of course. I believe every girl on the threshold of marriage battles them."

"Do you still have them?"

"No, I do not." Lydia's countenance showed peaceful confidence. "You know why?"

"Please tell me."

"I remembered what kind of man Papa is. He is unlike most Jewish men in Bethlehem. For he is a man of high honor, loving and caring for Mama, you, Miriam, Abigail, Anna, and me as people, not as his property. Therefore, I knew he would pick husbands for us who would not be concerned if we burnt their food or if we produced sons for them, but they would care more about our character and our hearts."

I turned back to face my sister. "I do think Papa found that man for you when he promised you to Matthew."

Lydia smiled and hugged me tightly. "I know he did, and he will find you the same kind of man, little sister. And I am sure of one thing—with as pure and good as your heart is, your husband will receive one of the most beautiful hearts in this whole nation.

I could not stop the smile even if I had wanted too. I took Lydia's hand and squeezed it. "I love you more than you know, Lydia. You always know what to say to ease my fears and doubts."

"I love you too, Hadassah. Before we seek sleep for the night, I must say one more thing, and I want you to do what I say. You are only eleven years old—you still have two years of your childhood left. Enjoy these years and do not worry about something that is so far in the future. You are only a little girl for so long and then a woman for the rest of your life. Be a silly, joyful, worry-free girl while you still can."

I crossed my eyes. "I will do my best, sister."

Lydia laughed. "Good! Now let us sleep."

CHAPTER 6

Not quite awake but believing I heard banging on the door, I hobbled into the family room trying not to stub my toe.

Papa came from his room.

"Did you hear that?"

He stumbled to the door just catching himself before he opened it.

"Yes, but I cannot think of who it would be. Who is it?" Papa asked.

"It is Jonathan, sir."

Papa unlatched the door and swung it open. "Jonathan, what is wrong?"

"It is the ewe, sir."

Papa shook his head. "She has not given birth yet?"

"No, sir. We have tried to make her comfortable. But she has now begun thrashing and bleating uncontrollably. I fear we might have a breech birth."

I touched Papa's arm. "We must go to her."

"You are right, Daughter." Papa rubbed his face with vigor. "Let us gather the things we might need, and we will be on our way."

The bleating echoed in the night sky before we even saw the ewe. My heart could not take the pitifulness, and I ran the rest of the way.

"Andrew! How is she?"

"She seems to be in a lot of pain." He stroked the ewe in comfort.

I knelt beside her face, petting, talking softly to soothe her. Papa and Jonathan bent down at the other end, and Papa checked the ewe.

"You are right, Jonathan. The lamb is breech. We need to work fast." Papa took out all of the tools and rags we brought. His skillful, quick hands showed the experience he had as a shepherd. "I need to pull its rear legs out from under him while he's still inside the ewe and then pull him out. Be ready to assist me."

The sweat poured from Papa's face as he strained to pull each leg forward. "The legs are out. I am going to pull the lamb out the rest of the way."

He began pulling the infant lamb out. Papa got the animal out halfway and stopped.

"It appears it is also a disproportionate birth, sir." Jonathan noted. "What are you going to do?"

Papa looked from me to Andrew and back at Jonathan and sighed. The lines etched in his weathered face showed how worried he was. Finally, the Papa I knew appeared. He sat up straight and began speaking with a steady voice that commanded authority. "I have to open her up more. We must act fast. The lamb's source of oxygen could already be broken." The wicked gleam of the knife contrasted with the peaceful light of the moon reflected off it.

Papa performed the act, and the ewe bleated in pain. I held her steady and spoke in soft tones. "Hold on girl, Papa knows what to do, as always."

"There. She is opened as much as she can be. I am going to pull the lamb out the rest of the way."

Papa began pulling. I gasped when he winced. "Papa, what is wrong?"

"The lamb's hind leg broke. He is sure to be maimed. Hadassah, I want you to prepare your heart. There is a great chance we will lose mother and lamb."

I could feel my pulse ringing in my ears. "No! Papa, please save them!"

"I am trying my best, my daughter. It is in Yahweh's hands."

Finally, one last pull and the lamb came out, revealing his oxygen source had indeed broken.

Papa handed the lamb to Jonathan. It was clear to all of us the lamb was alive, but barely.

"How's the ewe?" Papa asked me.

My tears mixed with the streaks of dirt on my cheeks. "Her breathing has become labored and erratic." I took a deep breath and looked down at the almost lifeless ewe. "She's not going to make it."

Papa put his hand to his head in distress and released an exhale that matched my own. "Move away from the ewe, Hadassah."

I could not move. Papa's words seemed like they were a million miles away as I felt outside of my body, witnessing the scene from above.

"Daughter! Move away from the ewe!"

I felt rough calloused hands grasp my arms and help me rise. I looked up at Andrew as we moved away from the dying sheep. Sobs shook my body as I watched the ewe thrash and gasp for breath. Andrew's arm never left my shoulders, giving me the solace I desperately needed in the most horrific moment of my life. In what seemed like an eternity, but was only mere seconds, the sheep took one final gasping breath and died. Papa looked at me, his eyes sad but strong. He had suffered this loss many times. With a shake of his head, he passed the mantle, the burden all shepherds shouldered to me. I clung to Andrew but looked at my father drawing from his strength. *"Tetelstai,"* I whispered.

I now understood why it appeared the weight of the world sat on Papa's shoulders every time sheep died. Uttering the death proclamation was a different kind of pain I'd had yet to experience. It took all of the strength I had left to speak that small word that held so much meaning.

Papa looked up to the stars. His mouth moved, forming words that could not be heard. "Give me strength, Abba!" The guttural plea echoed into the black of the night. I jumped in Andrew's arms. I did not expect Papa's cry of anguish. This was not how my Papa handled difficult situations. He was strong and steady like a mighty oak tree. Papa knelt down and picked up the dreadful knife. "Give me the lamb, Jonathan."

I watched as the hireling handed the lamb to Papa.

"Papa!" I broke free from Andrew's embrace. "What are you doing!?"

"Daughter, I must." His voice begged me to see reason. "He is barely breathing, and his leg is broken. He is in a lot of pain and his source of nourishment just died."

My heart threatened to leave the protection of my chest. My mind, which had knowledge of the ways of nature and a flock, knew Papa was right. He had always told me the words in Ecclesiastes were true. To everything, there was a season, even death. But my soul cried out to my mind, contradicting what I had been taught. It was not this lamb's season.

"I know, but Papa, I believe it would be a mistake. This lamb has a purpose—just as you have told me about every other lamb."

"Hadassah." Papa put his hands on my shoulders. I could see the tears soaking his grey beard. "This is why I asked God to give me strength. I knew the pain you would bear, and I was unsure if I could bear watching you. The love you have for your flock has made you forget what I have taught you, the aspects of being a shepherd no one wants to talk about. This lamb is maimed, it is barely breathing, and it is a male lamb that will never be fit for sacrifice. What purpose could it possibly have?" Papa pulled me into his embrace and held me as he did when I was a little girl. "I know this is more than you can take," he whispered in my ear. "Andrew, please take her back to the cabin to her mother."

Once again Andrew's arms surrounded me, but I jerked away from his grip. "No, Papa!" I begged God my sobs would not cause me to lay prostrate. "Please listen to me as you have asked me to listen to you! I do not know this lamb's exact purpose. But I know and truly believe he has one."

Papa stared at me and stroked his beard. I had never blatantly defied him before nor spoken to him in a disrespectful fashion. I stared back as he weighed if I was sincere, in a deep state of shock, or just a sad fool.

"You have never taken such a tone with me, even when you were angry. I do not know what is driving your passion, Hadassah, but even if I let it live, it has to have nourishment now. We do not have time to see if one of the other mother ewes would take him as her own. We have to act quickly."

The faintest root of hope sprouted in my heart. "I'll attend to the lamb."

"You will take care of it and feed it every four hours?"

"Yes, I will." I stood tall and felt my chin lift in determination.

"If you do this, you cannot neglect any of your other duties. This is a great responsibility. Are you sure can completely commit to it?"

"I can, Papa, I promise."

"Very well, Daughter, I will permit it. I pray it has a purpose as you say." Papa's words were simple, but I knew what was in his heart.

He doubted the lamb would live through the night.

Papa swung the cabin door open to Mama's frantic pacing.

"Samuel, Hadassah! Where have you be—" Mama stopped in mid-sentence. Her brown eyes grew wide, swallowing most of her face. I could only imagine how Papa and I must look. In the years Papa and Mama had been married, a hireling never sought Papa in the middle of the night. Now here we stood. A mix of blood, dirt, and tears and me holding a pathetic looking lamb.

Mama reached out to touch Papa and then withdrew her hands to touch her face. "Husband, what has happened?"

"The ewe strained for too long. When it came time to deliver the lamb, he was breech and too large for the small ewe to handle. I had to pull the lamb out. In the process, his right hind leg and his source of oxygen broke in the womb, so he is having trouble breathing. But the ewe had no strength left, and she died." Papa threw his hands in the air and fell into a nearby chair.

Poor Mama looked from Papa to me, trying to digest the gravity of the news. "Did anyone touch the dead ewe?"

Papa shook his head. "No. When the ewe's breathing became labored and erratic, we stepped away and let her die in peace. Jonathan and Andrew will keep watch over her body to make sure no wild animals come after it, and then, Jonathan will go get Julius the Roman farmer to bury the ewe at sunup."

Mama's eyes rested on the animal I cradled. I knew what was coming. "What of the lamb? It looks like it will die as well. Hadassah, take that animal out of the house at once!"

"He will not die, Mama."

CRACK! My cheek stung with my mother's rebuke."Do not defy me, child!" Her voice held the perfect mixture of panic and anger. "If that animal dies in here, our house will become unclean!"

Papa jumped from the chair—posture stiff like a shepherd's staff and voice as tight as twine. "Rachel! Listen to the child."

I tried to keep the tears from streaming down my face, but it could not be helped. Mama had never slapped me before. But the thought of our house becoming defiled was too much. Not only was it forbidden in the Law of God, but it would bring dishonor on Papa's household. And in the eyes of other Jews, since it was the woman's duty to keep the household pleasing to the Law, it would be Mama's fault. "I am sorry, Mama. I am not trying to defy you. I just have this feeling in my spirit that Yahweh wants this lamb to live."

Mama's soft hand touched my cheek it had just slapped. "Daughter, your love for your flock runs deep. I know your heart breaks anytime one of your sheep is in pain or in distress. But you have to face these kinds of things are a way of life. The lamb is maimed, unfit for sacrifice. What purpose would God have for him?"

I looked down at the lamb I held. Its body confirmed the fact it was near death, but the eyes that held mine were strong and alert. My heart stirred within me. I had to fight for this lamb. "It might not have a purpose that is obvious to people, but a purpose we could never think or imagine. A purpose that Yahweh could only orchestrate."

Mama sat down. "I do not know how to respond to such an answer, my child."

After a moment of silence between Mama and me, Papa spoke. "Rachel, my love, Hadassah and I will sleep outside with the lamb. Will you please ready our bedrolls while we change?"

"Yes, my husband."

Mama had the bedrolls ready when Papa and I returned. "Burn our clothing. We will not wear them again."

"I am going outside. Bye, Mama." I stepped into the cool night and waited for Papa, but I could still hear Mama's tight and short whispers.

"Do you think our daughter is right?"

"I don't know. The lamb will either live, and his purpose will be revealed in due time, or he will die, and our daughter will have a difficult lesson to learn."

To my surprise, I heard a sob come from Mama's lips. "But Samuel, you know the Law better than I do. If that lamb dies, you know what must happen. I do not want our daughter to feel that burden or disgrace."

Silence.

"Yes, I know. If Andrew or Jonathan come at the midday meal tomorrow, then know they will be tending to the flock until our seven-day purification period is over."

More sobs came from Mama. "I love you, Samuel."

"Oh, the love I have for you. Goodbye, my wife."

Silent heaves weighted my chest. The pain I was inflicting on Papa and Mama was so great, it could have killed me. But I could not turn away from this calling to give this lamb a chance. I knew this chance would bear unimaginable fruit.

Papa walked out of the cabin. “Come, Daughter.” I followed him into the darkness and to an unknown fate.

I held the baby lamb close, doing all I could do to keep it warm. Papa slept on the bedroll next to me. The Lord was so merciful for giving me a caring Papa who would go to great lengths for his daughter. If the animal died while I was holding it, then I would become unclean. Papa would become unclean as well because he would have to bury the lamb to protect us from wild animals. Once Papa buried the lamb, he and I would enter a seven-day purification period that all Jews must go through if they became unclean. We would leave all of society, go where no person lived so the risk of others becoming unclean would not be present. Seven days, the desolate wilderness would be our home. On the specific days God commanded, we would wash our bodies thoroughly. After the seven days were through, we could go back to living with our family and other Jews. But the shame and dishonor of being unclean would remain with us all our days. I did not take the sacrifice Papa made for me lightly.

The animal still struggled, but I did not doubt it would live. I knew this deep within my being. The lamb and I were connected.

I checked the makeshift bandage Papa had made from the hem of his tunic. It held the leg in place. The goatskins I filled with milk from one of the ewes that had just delivered held the nutrients the animal would need. I coaxed a few more drops of milk into him. His weak suckle should have discouraged me, but strength coursed through my every pour.

I looked up at the stars, the same stars Abraham looked at hundreds of years ago. If Yahweh could give Abraham and Sarah a son in their old age, then he could also breathe life into this lamb no one else believed would live.

I cradled the lamb's face. "Listen to me, my little lamb. Papa and Mama say you will die. People may say you have no purpose, or that you cannot even do what a male lamb is born to do because you are not perfect or without blemish. They are wrong. You will live, and through a maimed lamb, Yahweh will have a divine purpose. You will not atone for the sins of this nation, but in haste you will fulfill the Lord's purpose, being the only lamb to be in the presence of a monumental event in history."

A quiet reverence surrounded me. Had I just proclaimed a prophecy? In haste, he will fulfill God's purpose. In haste ...

Haste?

An invisible radiance warmed my cheeks. "I shall call you Haste."

Yawning, I snuggled down in my blankets and pulled Haste close to my side. "Do not worry, my Haste. I will always take care of you. I will never leave you nor forsake you."

"Baa ... Baa ..."

I rolled over, trying to quiet the nagging dream. But the consistent bleating combined with a fuzzy head nuzzling my side woke me up to reality.

I sat up as fast as David's sling. There in the pinks and blues of the morning light sat Haste. A completely different lamb. Joy filled my heart and soft giggles escaped my lips. I picked up the lamb and held him tight, hoping he could feel the champion he had in me.

"Papa! Wake up! Haste is going to be okay! Haste is going to live!"

Papa groaned and rubbed his neck. "Why must you yell, Daughter? And who in the Kingdom of David is Haste?"

I grabbed the goatskin of milk, laughing as the animal gulped the liquid down. "The lamb, Papa, I named him Haste."

Papa's head snapped in my direction. His face bellied the amazement he felt as the lamb sucked on the goatskin at a rapid pace. "So he lived! Wait ... Hadassah, you named a maimed lamb Haste?"

Once again, the joy I felt escaped in laughter. Bethlehem would probably think me a fool today because the joyous giggles would not cease. But I did not care. Haste was alive, his season new, fresh, and full of promise as the morning dew. "Yes, Papa. I do not know his purpose, but maimed or not, Yahweh has one, even though we might not see it now. Someday in haste, he will fulfill it."

Papa stared at me. Whether he thought I was a lunatic or wise beyond my years, I did not know. The time he took to blink rivaled the forty years our ancestors spent in the wilderness. Then, as if he saw a glimpse of the Promised Land, a smile of peace and hope covered his face. He pulled out the horn of oil shepherds always carried and gently anointed my lamb's head. "Haste—welcome to our flock."

CHAPTER 7

Much to everyone's surprise, but not mine, Haste grew strong and healthy, regardless of how he dragged his right hind leg. He followed me everywhere—even when I was not feeding him, he was by my side. My care for my flock could not be faulted, I was steadfast and determined. I loved my flock, and I determined I would give them my best, but it was obvious to all there was a special place in my heart for Haste. This became more apparent as my people's most reverent observance came upon us—Passover.

"Hadassah, go through the bread baskets. I've separated the leavened and the unleavened baskets, but please make certain they aren't mixed. I don't want any leavened bread to be consumed on Passover," Mama instructed.

A smile came to my lips. Mama asked me to do this every year, and every year the bread was split to perfection. I picked up the baskets and settled down on my mat. Haste followed me and laid his head on my leg. Following him was the ram that would be the sacrifice for Papa's family.

Imitating Haste, he laid his head on my other leg. I looked at both lambs and shuddered.

"Is something wrong, Hadassah?" Lydia asked with a smirk.

I huffed in exasperation. "First, you know what troubles me, Lydia. Second, I know we do not always understand God's ways, but why must the sacrificial lamb be in our house?"

"Because God commands it." Mama's voice was firm and resolute. I knew I was supposed to accept that and move on. Jewish women were expected to do what was commanded of them and not ask questions. But I did not accept that legalistic belief. Questioning Yahweh's commandments did not mean I rejected them—I wanted to understand them.

"My mind can't comprehend it, though. I'm emotionally bonded with my flock. To bring the ram into our home, become close to it, and then eat it after the priest has slit its throat is morbid."

Mama's face flushed, and I knew the cause was not the heat flowing from the bread. "Hadassah! We must not talk of our people's holy ritual so crassly!"

"But, Mama, that's what happens!" Lydia giggled and continued to knead the dough. "Hadassah, you did bring Haste home and are close to him."

I rolled my eyes. "That's different. I don't have to worry about his throat getting slit and then being forced to eat him."

"Hadassah!"

Lydia and I laughed at our horrified mother. I picked up Haste and kissed him dramatically on the head. "No, you don't have to worry, you will be safe and sound by my side always!" I cooed in his face as if he were a baby.

Haste bleated in joy and nuzzled my leg. Lydia smiled, shaking her head. “I still cannot believe Papa is allowing you to take Haste with us to Jerusalem.”

“He must go. Haste has not been weened yet.”

“Surely he would nurse from one of the other ewes.”

I smiled and cocked my head. “Nay, sister. Papa and I tried. He will only nurse when I feed him with a goatskin of milk.”

“That is the strangest lamb I have ever seen.” Lydia teased.

I gasped and covered Haste’s ears. “Shh, he can hear you!”

Lydia rolled her eyes. “Now I know where the lamb gets it.”

Once again, I gasped and placed my hand on my chest. I grabbed a piece of bread out of my basket and threw it at her.

“Daughters! Please, I have taught you better. It is irreverent to toss the Passover bread in jest.”

Lydia chuckled. “Mama, I will be married in less than two weeks. You know you will miss this.”

Tears filled Mama’s eyes. “More than you know.”

We fell silent, allowing each other to ponder and grieve the changes that were to come. I continued searching the basket for the unleavened bread. “Oh no ...” I said slowly. “Mama! There is bread with yeast mixed in the unleavened bread!”

Mama jumped up from her loom. “That cannot be! I was ever so careful.”

“I am teasing, Mama!”

She looked from me to Lydia, a smile slowly forming on her lips, and my heart felt light as my no-nonsense Mama leaned on her loom, happy laughter escaping from her lips. Lydia and I joined our mother laughing, and anyone who passed by the small home heard joyful giggles coming from the Jewish women of the house.

CHAPTER 8

Knock ... Knock ... Knock ...

"That must be your sisters." Mama told Lydia and me.

Every Wednesday, Mama, my sisters, and I would go to the city to purchase what we needed for our households and visit my grandfather, Mama's papa. If nothing was needed, we would go straight to visit my grandfather. Grandfather owned and ran an inn in the city of Bethlehem. Thankfully, business was strong and steady, but Wednesday afternoons were slow. Mama's mother died in childbirth when her youngest brother was born. Being the only daughter in her family, Mama felt it was her duty to make sure her father was taken care of—her six brothers had their own households to lead and see to. They visited Grandfather once or twice a month, but that was not enough for Mama's liking.

As we walked to the city, we would talk of our domestic duties and how my nieces and nephews were faring. When we arrived at the marketplace, the six of us did what we always did on market day—divide and conquer.

I walked to the booth selling yarn. I was weaving a rug and needed blue yarn to complete my work. I waited in line and stepped up to the merchant. "Good day, sir, I need blu—"

I gasped as the wind was knocked out of me, falling forward. Steadying myself with the booth, I looked up to see who or what knocked into me with such force. A large man spoke to the merchant. I spoke Hebrew and Aramaic, but I couldn't understand the language this man was speaking.

Greek ... He was a *gentile*.

"I do not care how much your wife needs my goods, I will not serve a Greek dog before a Jew, especially a young Jewess who you have treated so savagely." The merchant's Greek was broken, but the foreigner received the message. I watched his eyes become hard as flint. He slammed his hand down on the front of the booth.

Not wishing a for a brawl to begin, I stepped forward. "Nay, I do not want any trouble. The man can go before me. I can wait."

Breathing a sigh of relief, the transaction took place with no one receiving a blow, I stepped forward after the Greek left. "Thank you for your patience and kindness, my lady. I did not have any for him."

"I did not want any fighting on my account. I think he would have destroyed your booth if I did not intervene."

The merchant shook his head. "You may have squelched that fire, my lady, but the sad truth is tensions are high between Jew and Gentile. It is not a matter of *if* fighting will happen, but who and *when* the flame will be ignited. Things are not as peaceful in the city as they are in the sheep pastures."

I refused to begin a debate with this man. I took the excess money and my purchase. "Good day, sir." I nodded and smiled.

If he thought I was insolent, so be it. I made my way to the front of the city's synagogue to meet Mama and my sisters. The place of worship glistened in the sunlight as the white marble boasted of its beauty. As I got closer, I saw my mother and sisters huddled in an intense conversation. "What happened at the booth where you bought yarn, Hadassah?" Lydia asked as she saw me approach.

"I will explain later, but let us not talk of it in front of Grandfather. His anger may cause him to do something foolish."

Mama shook her head. "He is a Judahite for certain. He is courteous to uncircumcised foreigners, of course, since they frequent the inn, but if they take advantage of a young Jewish woman's weakness, he becomes a different man. He would have avenged Dinah's virtue along with Judah, Simeon, Levi, and the rest of the brothers if he were one of Jacob's sons. But please remember to share with me and Papa what happened, Hadassah. I did not see what took place, but Lydia told me it looked dangerous."

"I will, Mama."

We passed down the road until the market stalls were behind us and all that remained were the tall clay buildings. Grandfather's inn sat by itself, away from houses so the weary traveler would know where they could seek out lodging. We entered the inn, and Grandfather beamed as he saw us. "The apples of my eye have entered!" he bellowed to his guests.

"Hello, Papa," Mama said as she kissed his cheek. "How do you fare this afternoon?"

"Well, well. How is that Benjaminite treating you?"

Mama chuckled. "Papa, will you ever call him Samuel?"

"Never. I must keep my only son-in-law humble. Especially since he's not from our tribe."

"Well, Papa, he would tell you he is from the tribe whose mother was Rachel, Jacob's favorite wife."

"Ah, yes, but our tribe will bring forth the chosen one, and you cannot get any better than that." Grandfather's eyes twinkled in jest.

"Well, I do not think his tribal heritage offends you too much—you did give him your blessing to marry your only daughter."

Grandfather chuckled. No matter what he said, everyone knew how much he loved and respected our father. "Come, come, show me your purchases from today."

Mama, my sisters, and I laid out what we had bought that day.

"Clay, I see, Abigail. Is Joshua beginning another project?"

"Yes, Grandfather. The pottery business is steady, thanks to a certain innkeeper." Abigail grinned.

Grandfather waved off the compliment. "Ah, Granddaughter, I just point my customers in your direction. It is Yahweh's blessing and Joshua's talent that is responsible for the business's success.

"And Lydia, that blue fabric is beautiful. What are you making, my dear?"

"I am finishing a coat for Matthew, and I thought this blue fabric would look so becoming on the trim. I know it is not customary for the bride to give the groom a wedding gift, but I wanted to anyway."

"I think that is a fine idea!"

"You do? You are such a traditional Jewish man."

"There is a difference between being traditional and legalistic, Granddaughter. If what you are doing is not displeasing to our God, then it is fine. I think it is beautiful you want to do something special for your betrothed."

Lydia beamed at our grandfather. Losing my grandmother had softened him over the years. He was by no means a tyrant, but when Grandmother was alive, he could be gruff. Now it was as if he had taken on so many of my grandmother's traits to honor her memory—good humor, tenderness, and thoughtful intention.

Grandfather's eyes rested on me. "Well, Hadassah, it is unexpected for you to have a domestic purchase."

"You are right, Grandfather. I need more practice on my loom. I have delayed purchasing what I need until today."

"There is the Hadassah I know and love—spending more time in the sheep pasture than learning how to run a household," Grandfather said with a chuckle.

I rolled my eyes and laughed. "In truth, if I had a say, I would not marry at all and work in the pasture for the rest of my years."

Grandfather stared at me and stroked his salt and pepper beard. Finally, he spoke.

"My granddaughter, come with me. I want to show you something."

I followed my grandfather across the large dining hall to the window. "You see the stable cave?"

I looked from my grandfather to the stable cave and then back at him. "Grandfather, I have seen this stable cave many times. Why do you show me this?"

"You may have seen this stable cave many times, but there is one thing you do not know."

I tipped my head to the side, truly perplexed. "Of what are you speaking?"

Grandfather put his arm around my shoulders. "This stable cave has a special place in my heart. Every night after my customers have gone to their slumber and the great hall is cleaned and ready for the next day, I go to this stable cave in the quietness of the night. I pray for my family, reflect on the days I have lived, and ponder on what's to come. This cave has become a comforting friend to this old man over the years."

"I am pleased this stable cave has been such a peaceful reprieve for you over the years, but what does it have to do with me? I know you must have a word of wisdom to bestow on me." My voice held no emotion. I was simply vexed from people trying to persuade me that what I wanted was not really what I wanted.

"Many thanks for not containing your joy, Granddaughter," Grandfather said dryly.

I gave him a cheeky smile as he continued. "It is not so much a wise word as it is a truth I learned, and I want to bestow it on you. When I was a young man, I would have been content to run this inn for the rest of my days. And being a man, I could have. I know it does not seem fair that a man has more freedom than a woman, but as you know, that is our way and the way it must be. But the day your grandmother walked into this inn—your great-grandfather's inn in those years—my heart dropped to my knees. I have heard other Jewish people say nothing good could come from Galilee. Well, they never met your grandmother. Full lips that looked like crimson, the blackest and shiniest hair I have ever seen that cascaded down her back and stopped at her hips—she is the reason you have all those beautiful raven curls. Out of all my grandchildren, you look the most like her."

I smiled at my grandfather with a warm heart, truly touched by the comparison.

"Soon after your grandmother and I married, I began making my way to the stable cave. I found the best place for me to rest and process the day's events was away from the place that occupied and consumed my thoughts. Even after your grandmother began giving me my children, I still came to the cave under the stars. And now my children have children, my precious grandchildren. And slowly over the years, I began to understand that without my wife, my children, my grandchildren, prayer, and thinking about what is to come, my life would be empty and void. I would not have had anyone to share what comes next. I would not have had anyone to pray for, which would be tragic, because I believe there is more purpose in prayer when you have someone to pray for. I would have missed out on so much if I had decided to never wed. My children would have never existed, my grandchildren would have never walked on this earth, and the memories I ponder when I am in that cave fill me with immense joy. Now, I know there are people who say you should marry because it is a woman's duty, but I am here to tell you to open your heart to a possibility much sweeter than that."

I put my other arm around my grandfather and embraced him. "Thank you, Grandfather. I will think on what you just said."

A possibility sweeter than that. Could it be true?

CHAPTER 9

"Come, Hadassah, share with your mother and me what happened in the marketplace," Papa called to me after dinner. Lydia and Haste followed me from our room, eager to hear what happened too. I settled on my pillow and looked at my parents.

"I went to the booth that was selling yarn and—"

"*You* bought yarn?" Papa said, with one eyebrow almost reaching his hairline and the other drooping to his eye.

"Samuel," Mama warned.

"My apologies, Hadassah. Go on."

"Well, when it was my turn, I stepped up to the vendor's booth and had started telling him what I needed when I was shoved to the side by a man who spoke Greek. An angry conversation began between the vendor and the man, but it did not take me long to see the Greek was a drunkard and perhaps did not even realize what he was doing or saying. To keep the two men from coming to blows, I allowed the Greek to finish his transaction."

"Were you hurt, Hadassah?" Mama asked.

I shook my head. "No, the push only took the breath from my lungs for a few seconds, and then, I was fine." I shifted my focus to my father. "But, Papa, the vendor made the strangest comment to me. He said tensions are high between Jews and Gentiles, and it is not a matter of if conflict will arise, but a matter of when and who ignites the flame. Is this true, Papa?"

Papa sighed deeply. "It is. We are very blessed to live in the country, as we are sheltered from the rising hostility. But we do need to be aware of what is happening with our people and the rest of the world. I have heard from multiple people of the hatred that is growing between Jew and non-Jew." Papa stood and walked to the fire that was crackling in the fireplace. He stared at it as if he was trying to make sense of it all himself so he could be a comfort to his family.

"I believe what makes our people anxious is we have not heard from God in years. They wonder when God will give us the Messiah he promised. Some are starting to doubt. And Gentiles are starting to mock. And we all know how some Jews think themselves superior to others because we are the chosen race. It is the perfect combination for trouble."

Papa turned back around to face us. "I by no means want you to live in fear. You must live and go about your normal routines. But when you are in the marketplace, you must be aware of who is around you. Hadassah, you handled today's situation with grace and wisdom, and I am very proud of you. Remember, the most powerful way to deflate troubling and hostile situations is through kindness and compassion."

Papa looked at his family scurrying about, preparing for their journey, and smiled. It was his favorite time of year—Passover. Miriam, Anna, and Abigail would be with their husbands' families when we arrived in Jerusalem, but at least we could all travel together. Bethlehem was five miles south of Jerusalem, so we would set up camp for the night and finish our sojourn when the sun rose the next morning.

Once everything was in order, Papa gathered his most treasured possessions—as he called us. "Listen, family, we need to begin our journey now to ensure we will make it to camp by nightfall. May Yahweh put his hand of protection on us."

The men lifted their wives and young children up on their donkeys, and we began our trek to the holy city, where we would engage in the most sacred act a Jew had the honor to perform.

As my family traveled, many conversations floated in the air. Miriam told Anna about the vibrant colors she chose to create a rug with her loom—as bright as Joseph's coat, she declared. Abigail and Lydia discussed Lydia's wedding and the finishing touches Matthew had left to complete on their little home. Everyone was enjoying someone else's company. Except me. With Haste's limp, he and I were several feet behind the caravan. Papa finally noticed how far away we were from the family. "Daughter," he called. "Please pick up Haste and come with the rest of the family. It is not safe for a young woman to be by herself on these roads."

I scooped my lamb into my arms and walked toward my family. I fell into place with Anna and her husband, David. David was a practical and stoic man with legalistic beliefs, and he was not shy in letting his opinions known. I braced myself for what was about to come.

"I do not understand why you brought that crippled lamb." David's lowered brow and pursed lips made me feel like a fool. I knew I was not, but that knowledge did not keep the feelings of being small at bay. I wished I was walking with Miriam, who was always a nurturer and a peacemaker.

I looked at Anna, who lowered her head, refusing to speak out against her husband. I fought my urge to shake my head at Anna's submissiveness to her husband. I believed I could be respectful to a man while having my own convictions, and I was not afraid to voice them, even if David's words made me feel lesser.

"First of all, Haste is not crippled. If he was, he would not be able to walk at all. Secondly, he came because he is not weaned yet." I cocked my head, and a small smile came to my lips. "All of which you knew."

David shook his head. "Does Samuel allow such disrespect in his household? My Anna would never talk to me in that fashion."

I shook my head. Papa would never constitute disrespect from his wife or daughters. But Papa did not treat his wife and daughters like dim-witted cows. He treated us with dignity and respect, valuing any wisdom we had to offer.

David smirked and took my silence and lack of explanation as confirmation of his opinion. While Papa's character was true to how I perceived it, he would thrash me if I ever voiced my truest thoughts.

"Well, at least you do not have another disrespectful remark. I know you say God has some kind of purpose for your lamb, but I do not see it. The sooner you give up this childish fantasy, the better." He gestured toward Haste. "It can barely walk, and it is not fit for sacrifice. I think it would have been a mercy to that lamb if your father had done what he intended the night it was born and slit its throat. The animal is dead weight. Nothing more."

I held Haste tighter as my heart dropped at such a cruel and thoughtless remark. I felt a fire fill my cheeks and neck. I looked at my pregnant sister for any sign of shock or support, but as usual, Anna's head was down, refusing to contradict or reprimand her husband, even if he was talking to her sister like a stray dog no one cared about.

My glare held David's eyes. "Do not speak such things ever again." My seething tone and the hard glint in my eyes showed David he went too far. He would never apologize to a woman, but his loss of words told me I had made my point. I moved up to the front of the caravan to converse with family I actually enjoyed.

We made it to the outskirts of Jerusalem just before nightfall and set up camp. My papa and brothers-in-law began collecting twigs and branches to make a fire for warmth, while my mama, my sisters, and I prepared the food and laid down the bedrolls. My nieces and nephews played with each other, and when all was accomplished, Papa blessed the food, and we all ate together in contentment. After we ate, we rested from our journey and enjoyed each other's company.

I sat against a fig tree and watched as the beautiful pinks and oranges of dusk painted the sky. My family was close enough that I could see their happy expressions but far enough away to give me some solitude. There were so many personalities and dynamics, and yet we all fit together perfectly. Well, besides David, perhaps.

I smiled as I watched Papa take Mama's hand and kiss it. He leaned over and whispered something in Mama's ear, and she laughed in delight. Like a sudden rush of wind, I understood why my family was so unified. Because Papa and Mama made sure of it.

My musings were interrupted as my nephew Thaddeus climbed up on my lap. “Hello, to you too, Thaddeus.” I grinned down in the little boy’s large black eyes that resembled coal.

“Hi, ’Dasa. What are you doing?”

“Oh, I’m just sitting here, watching our family.”

Thaddeus’s nose wrinkled in an adorable fashion. “Why?”

I shifted my nephew in my lap. “It is just fascinating to watch the different conversations and wonder what everyone is talking about.”

“Oh. How’s Haste?” he asked, changing thoughts quickly, as do most four-year-olds.

“He’s fine. I think all of this travel has worn him out,” I said, looking at the sleeping lamb by my feet.

“Can I feed him next time?”

“Oh, I think Haste would enjoy that.” We were silent for a few moments until my inquisitive nephew asked yet another question.

“’Dasa?”

“Hmm?”

“What do you think Haste’s purpose is?”

The little boy asked me this question from time to time, and I always had the same answer for him.

“I do not know, Nephew, but I know Yahweh has something special for Haste.”

“How do you know?”

I paused for a moment. He had never asked this question before, but I had an answer for him as if God whispered it to me. “Thaddeus, whenever you are the shepherd, your sheep become your family. You possess a love for them like a mother loves her children. The shepherd knows his sheep. The flock’s heart becomes connected to their shepherd’s heart. And because of that, your heart will know when one of your lambs is particularly special and will be used by God."

"But Haste is maimed."

I smiled at Thaddeus. His statement mirrored David's, but Thaddeus said this in innocence, not arrogance. "All the more reason God will use Haste."

Thaddeus pondered that comment and then changed the subject again.

"'Dasa, will you be sad when Papa and me get your flock?"

I held the nephew I adored a little tighter. "I will be sad. But I will also be happy. You know why?"

"Why?"

"Thaddeus, I love you so much. I will not have to worry, because they will be with you, and I know you will love and protect the flock."

Thaddeus threw his chubby arms around my neck. "I will, 'Dasa! You do not have to worry. I will keep them safe!"

This was how Miriam found us. "Well now, what a sweet sight this is."

"Oh, Mama," Thaddeus said with excitement. "When I am shepherd, I will take care of the flock!"

Miriam smiled at her small son. "I know you will. In fact, I think you should go show Grandfather how you know how to use a sling now."

"Okay!"

My sister and I smiled as Thaddeus ran to Papa to show off his new skill.

"He adores you, you know." Miriam told me.

"I adore him as well."

"Thank you for acting so gracious when he talks about inheriting the flock. I know it is not an easy subject for you."

"Well, as I told Thaddeus, I will be sad, but also happy knowing that he will love and take good care of the flock."

"That he will. It is all he talks about some days. He reminds me of you."

I grinned at my sister.

Miriam stared at the fire and said casually, "I heard your conversation with David."

I sighed. "I know I was not kind, but when anyone belittles Haste, I become very protective."

"He should not have said what he said, but you should have not disrespected him as you did. You best thank Yahweh that I heard you and not Papa."

"But that is what I do not understand, Miriam. Papa would never talk down to a woman the way David does. It is not that *what* he says is always wrong, but it is the *way* he says it."

"David and Papa are two different men. David is more traditional and ritualistic. Papa believes that men are the leaders and heads of the household, but women are an integral part of the household. As such, they should be respected and held in high esteem."

"Then why did Papa approve Anna's marriage to David?"

Miriam smiled tenderly. "Have you seen the way he looks at Anna? He adores her and she brings the out best from him. Anna loves him. Yes, he is opinionated and gruff, but he is just and fair. Papa saw what a good husband he would make despite his flaws. Because remember, Hadassah—we all have faults."

A crooked grin formed on my lips. "I certainly proved that."

Miriam took my hand. "Do not beat yourself up too much, little sister. David did bring it on himself," Miriam said with a wink.

I giggled. I loved Miriam's way of affirming my feelings, but gently showing me how I could do better. "I suppose I should apologize to David."

"I was hoping you would say that. I know it might not be enjoyable, but remember our sister is involved. Do it for our sister."

I nodded. "I'll do it for Anna."

CHAPTER 10

I rose and linked arms with my oldest sister and we walked to where our family was sitting. As we drew closer to the chatter, Thaddeus's joyous and innocent voice rang out. "It is my turn to ask the questions during the Passover feast, Grandfather!"

Papa smiled. "What a special and important role you hold this year, Thaddeus. Are you anxious?"

Thaddeus cocked his head to the side, thinking about the question Papa asked him. Finally, he spoke, "No, Grandfather, I like to talk."

My family's laughter rang out in the night air, amused at my nephew's pure honesty. I sat down on my mat, and once I got settled and looked up, my eyes locked with David's. "I am sorry," I mouthed. David lowered his head in uncharacteristic humility, and I knew all was forgiven—shocked, but relieved we put our differences behind us.

"Perhaps you could show us the questions you will be asking since the rest of us will not be present to see you preform your task?"

"I would love to, Grandfather! But how will I know when to ask the questions here?"

"I will say the words which will prompt you to ask the questions."

Thaddeus nodded. "Good idea." His face was serious and determined.

A faint smile formed on Papa's lips. "Very well, Grandson. The women in the household have just poured the second glass of wine and have taken their seats. Your time has come. Do you have something to say?"

"Yes, Grandfather. Why is this night different? Tonight, we are only eating unleavened bread, bitter herbs, and roasted meat. Why can we not eat other things?"

"Those are very good questions, Thaddeus. Please tell us why."

Thaddeus's nose scrunched in an adorable, confused fashion. "Grandfather, I am not supposed to answer the questions."

Papa chuckled. "I know, Grandson. During the Passover ritual you will not answer the questions you ask. But I want to know if you know why Passover is so significant to our people."

"I do, Grandfather, I do! Hundreds of years ago, a famine befell the whole land. Joseph, a man in Egypt who was second-in-command to Pharaoh, came up with a plan to feed all people so no one would die of starvation. But Joseph had a secret. He was not Egyptian. He was a Hebrew, a part of the Jewish race just like we are. When he was young, his ten older brothers sold him into slavery, because he was their father's favorite, and they hated Joseph because of it. Well, because of the famine, Joseph's brothers, the sons of Jacob, traveled to Egypt to request some of the grain stored for everyone in the land to share."

"You know the beginning of our history very well, Thaddeus." Papa praised. "What happened next?

"After Joseph made sure his brothers had changed, he revealed who he was, and they all forgave each other. Joseph told his brothers to gather their families, their youngest brother, Benjamin, and their father, Jacob, and bring them to Egypt to live so he could take care of them. The Lord blessed the family of Israel, and before Jacob died, he made his sons the heads of tribes—the tribes of Israel. Mama is from the tribe of Benjamin, and Papa is from the tribe of Judah. And because Papa is the head of the household, I am a Judahite too." Thaddeus gasped, his little lungs needing a break after saying so much in one breath.

"Son," Miriam said softly, "remember what we have talked about. When someone asks you a question, only give them the answer to what they have asked."

"But Mama, every story has a beginning. I have to tell the beginning, so everyone knows how we get to the ending."

Papa's eyes twinkled. "He is not wrong, Daughter."

Miriam rolled her eyes. "This child has an answer for everything. And I cannot fault him because he shares his thoughts with respect, and what he says always has merit." Miriam shook her head. "When he begins his studies of our laws, he's going to be much too clever and inquisitive for his own good."

Papa winked at Miriam. "This is all very good, Thaddeus. Tell us more."

"But skip to the important stuff, Thaddeus." Miriam told her son.

"Ah, but Mama!"

"Thaddeus, do as your mother says, Son." Mark told his first-born. He did not raise his voice, but my nephew knew better than to defy his father.

"Yes, Papa." Thaddeus looked at everyone around the campfire. "I am very glad you all know the middle part because Mama and Papa say I have to skip to the end."

I looked over at Miriam. She placed her hand over her mouth, and her eyes twinkled in amusement.

"Well, our God hated how his people were treated by the Egyptians. He picked a man named Moses to be the leader of the Israelites. God commanded Moses to go to Pharoah and demand he let the Hebrews go. But Pharoah refused. So, God caused plagues to happen to the Egyptians—bloody water, frogs, lice, flies, death of livestock, boils on their skin, hail from the sky, locusts, and darkness." Thaddeus's eyes were wide, and his hands moved like the wind. "But Pharaoh still did not let God's people go. So, God had to cause the saddest plague of all to happen.

"I do not like hearing about this last plague." Papa told his grandson.

"I do not either, but Pharaoh wouldn't listen!" Thaddeus said passionately, defending God. Thaddeus took a breath and raised his hand for emphasis. "All the first-born males would die by the angel of death. But so the angel of death would pass over the Children of Israel's houses, they put lambs' blood on their door posts. And the angel of death did not kill any Hebrews, just as God said."

"Pharaoh was sad because his son had died, so he allowed Moses to lead the children of Israel out of Egypt. But Pharaoh's heart filled with pride and anger, so he and his soldiers went after the Israelites. They chased them right up to the Red Sea. It looked like the Egyptians had won, but then through the power of God, Moses lifted his staff, and the Red Sea parted."

"Now, here comes the happy part of the story!" Thaddeus jumped up and down in excitement. "There was a perfect pathway for every single Hebrew to cross over to the other side. After every Hebrew was safely on the other side of the Red Sea, the Egyptians began to cross on the path through the water, but Moses lowered his staff, and the sea came down, crushing the whole Egyptian army. The children of Israel were safe and free. And that is how Passover came to be." Thaddeus nodded his head to emphasize the ending.

"That is wonderful, Thaddeus." Papa said. "Why don't you come over and sit on my knee?"

I watched my nephew settle on Papa's leg. "You are right, Grandson. That is how Passover came to be. But can you tell me why?"

"Yes, Grandfather." Thaddeus cuddled up to Papa. "We celebrate Passover to remember how God saved us from bondage. We celebrate Passover to remember where our people once were to appreciate where we are now. And the most important reason we celebrate Passover is to remember what God did for our ancestors, he can do for us."

Samuel sat silently listening to the intense conversation between his sons-in-law. He was surprised the women and children slept through the heated voices.

"I tell you, I am very close to losing my temper with the Romans. The humiliation and cruelty those dogs unleash on our people is maddening. They have little regard for our customs and the laws God gave us. They have been told and yet, still do not comprehend that we are the chosen people of the true living God," Miriam's husband lamented.

The other young men nodded their heads in agreement. "I long for the day the Messiah will rise up and avenge us. Rome will be crushed under his rule, and the Jews will be the exalted race in the world," David boasted.

The men added their agreement with "amen" and "from your lips to God's ears." Silence filled the night air as the men pondered the words that were just spoken.

"Samuel." Joshua's voice interrupted the contemplation. "You have not said much. What do you believe the Messiah's purpose will be on this earth?"

Samuel remained quiet for a moment. His sons-in-law were young and full of fire. Thirsty for bloodshed of the Romans and complete dominion over the corrupt empire. Samuel was once a young man, and he had the same arrogant and entitled views his sons did. But he was now an old man, and he had seen and learned much in his fifty years. His daughters' husbands would not want to hear the wisdom he had gleaned in his years. He would give them compassion and understanding, though, because they would learn what he had as they aged. Of this he was confident.

"I believe God's plan of redemption will not be the Messiah overthrowing the Roman government, but he will have a much more intricate purpose. I do not know what the Messiah will come to do, but I believe he will not only come to change the nation of Israel, but the whole world as well."

David stared at his father-in-law. "Surely, you do not mean the Gentiles!" he spat.

"I do, indeed," Samuel told David, his calmness contrasting with his son-in-law's incredulousness.

"Samuel, you cannot be serious," Joshua said with wide eyes.

"I am. Look throughout our history. God accepted many Gentiles as his own."

"Because they became Jews," Joshua reasoned.

Samuel chuckled softly. "It was not because they became Jews. God accepted them because they chose him. Those foreigners accepted our God as their one true God and began worshiping only him."

"But we are God's chosen people. We are set apart," Benjamin countered.

"Being set apart does not mean we are above every person and nationality. It means we are God's messengers, so people will come to know Yahweh through our nation—Jew and Gentile alike."

David shook his head. "I do not agree with you, Samuel. There may be a few who think as you do, but most Jews do not."

Samuel smiled and shrugged. They were thirsty for confrontation and debate just as many men were when they were deemed old enough to discuss and defend God's laws. The last thing he would do was engage in a debate with his young, hot-headed sons-in-law. It would accomplish nothing and complicate much. "Well, this is not the first time someone has disagreed with me, and it will not be the last."

The young men smiled in relief that they had not offended their father-in-law. They loved and respected him far too much for division. The men sought their rest so they could be rejuvenated for their journey. They would travel the rest of the way to Jerusalem starting at dawn, and then the next day, thousands of men would gather at the temple for the most important day of the year—Passover.

CHAPTER 11

I helped Mama, Lydia, my aunts, and my cousins prepare the food and set the table. We were in the house of Papa's Uncle Samuel, the man he was named after. The house was cleaned, and all the leavened bread had been removed from the house. Now the women cooked the food for the Passover ceremony, while every circumcised male eight years and older was at the temple offering the family's sacrifice.

I sat a place for Elijah in hopes the old prophet would make an appearance. I took in the house. All looked ready. The table was laden with bitter herbs and unleavened bread. Each table setting had four cups for the ritual wine we would partake of. The non-ritual wine sat on the mantel along with the water the men would use to wash their feet when they returned to the house. A separate pitcher was available for the entire household to wash their hands before they ate the Passover meal.

I felt pressure on my leg and looked down at Haste nuzzling my calf. I knelt and cuddled the animal. I could not imagine my life without Haste. He was such a loveable little companion. Several times throughout the day, he nuzzled my leg, showing me his affection and love. Despite his maimed leg, Haste was happy and loved life. I hugged Haste tight as I realized if he had been born a perfect lamb, at next year's Passover, he could have been the sacrifice. I sent a prayer of thanksgiving I would never have to worry about that.

A few minutes later, the men walked in the house, and on Papa's shoulders was the lamb that atoned for our family. Papa poured water on his feet and then placed the ram over the spit of the fire to roast. The other men washed their feet and then, one by one, the entire household washed their hands. We sat around the table with Uncle Samuel at the head and Papa at his right as the guest of honor.

Uncle Samuel looked at our family and raised his head and arms to the Heavens. "Blessed are you, O Lord our God who has created the fruit of the vine. Blessed are you, O Lord who kept us alive, sustained us, and enabled us to enjoy this season."

The ritual wine was passed around and poured in everyone's first cup. When every cup was filled, the elder Samuel spoke again. "I am the Lord, and I will bring you out from under the burdens of the Egyptians."

After Uncle uttered these words, every man, woman, and child drank the wine in their cup. When everyone had drunk their wine, Papa held up the bowl of vinegar for his uncle to dip the bitter herbs. He then took a piece of the bitter herb and passed the plate to Papa, and then Papa passed the platter to Mama. Once the whole household had a piece of the bitter herbs, we ate in unison.

I, along with Mama, Lydia, my aunts, and my cousins, took all the food off the table. As I passed my four-year-old cousin, Nathaniel, he was squirming in his seat, and I had to hide my grin. It was his turn to ask the questions, and he was ready for his part.

After we sat down and the second wine was poured, Uncle Samuel looked at his young grandson. His eyes sparkled at the boy's enthusiasm, but his face remained reverent. "Nathaniel, do you have something to say?"

"Yes, Grandfather. Why is this night different? Tonight, we are only eating unleavened bread, bitter herbs, and roasted meat. Why can we not eat other things?"

"Well, Grandson, there is a very good reason for that. Shall I tell you?"

Nathaniel bobbed his head.

I sat as I heard my great uncle recount the history of our people from Abraham to when Moses gave God's laws to Israel. It never ceased to amaze me how Israel came to be. What a mighty God I served! How God had intricately woven his plan throughout the Jewish people to me proved that he was the one true God.

When the head of the household finished sharing the Jewish history, I and the other women in the household put all the food back on the table, including the roasted lamb. Uncle Samuel explained the sacrifice of the unleavened bread and the roasted ram. Tears filled my eyes as my family joined their voices, singing the first part of the Hallel Psalms.

> *Praise ye the LORD. Praise, O ye servants of the LORD, praise the name of the LORD. Blessed be the name of the LORD from this time forth and for evermore. From the rising of the sun unto the going down of the same the LORD's name is to be praised. The LORD is high above all nations, and his glory above the heavens. Who is like unto the LORD our God, who dwelleth on high, Who humbleth himself to behold the things that are in heaven, and in the earth! He raiseth up the poor out of the dust, and lifteth the needy out of the dunghill; That he may set him with princes, even with the princes of his people. He maketh the barren woman to keep house, and to be a joyful mother of children. Praise ye the LORD.*

I let the beautiful words of God's majesty and provision settle over my heart and soul. When the hymn was over, my great uncle blessed the second cup of wine. "Blessed are you, O Lord our God, King of the universe, who has created the fruit of the vine ... I will rid you of their bondage."

With those words spoken, we washed our hands again, and the lamb, two kinds of vegetables, and two unleavened pieces of bread were served. "Blessed are you, O Lord our God, King of the universe, who brings forth bread from the earth. Blessed are you, O Lord our God, King of the universe, who has sanctified us with your commandments and commanded us to eat unleavened bread." Uncle Samuel broke the bread and then broke Papa's bread. Together they dipped the bread into the bitter herbs and in the lamb. Papa in turn assisted Mama, until every person helped the person on their right.

Uncle Samuel looked at our family with outstretched arms. "Now, let us partake of the Passover meal."

Nathaniel exhaled with relief. "Good! I thought we would never get to eat."

We all laughed at my cousin's innocent honesty, even Haste's bleats at my feet mixed with our laughter as if he knew like we did it would be a few years before my cousin understood the significance of what was happening. But then again, maybe Haste did know. He possessed a keen intuition I had never seen in any other lamb. The rest of the Passover ceremony went smoothly, leaving my family and me with thankful hearts for all God had done for us and our people.

I looked up at the beautiful sparkling stars that Abraham looked at hundreds of years ago as I dragged the tin bathtub into the house. I huffed and wiped the sweat from my brow. I was strong, but the size of the tub was too cumbersome for me. I left the tub in the doorway and walked to my room.

"Lydia," I whispered.

I listened as my sister groaned. "What, Hadassah?"

"I need your help."

Lydia sat up. "You do remember I am getting married tomorrow and need my sleep."

"I do remember, and if you do not help me, I will not be at your wedding."

Lydia's brows lowered in question. She rose from her bed and followed me into our main room. "Why are you bringing the tub in here at this hou— Hadassah! Have you not purified yourself yet?!"

I scrunched my lips and shook my head.

"Why?"

"Because it is stupid!"

Lydia's face distorted. I could tell she did not know whether to scold me or laugh. "Mama would thrash you if she overheard you blaspheming God's law in this way."

"I do not feel like I am blaspheming God. I am simply being honest. He created us, he gave women our monthly flows, and yet we are unclean when we have them." My hands flew in the air as I gave my passionate argument. "And do not get me started on what I think about blood coming out of a strange place, the cramps in my stomach, and mood swings! One second, I am crying, and the next second, I am euphorically happy! Look!" I pointed to my chin. "Look—every month this bump appears on my chin when I have my monthly flow. It hurts and only goes away after my menses are through. And now, now I must get a bath. Not just any bath, a specific bath with specific spices because that is the only way I can be clean to be around people again!"

Through my whole tirade Lydia stood silent, staring at me with her hand on her chin. Out of the corner of my eye I saw Haste start to venture out of my room. "Haste! Go back to bed now!"

"Why can he not be out here?"

"Because I do not want him to see me naked!" I cried.

Lydia lowered her head into her hand and massaged her temples. Her mouth was moving as she rubbed her forehead and eyes.

"What are you doing?"

"I am praying for the poor soul who will be your husband."

I put my hands on my hips. "Well, that is offensive."

I stared at Lydia, and she stared at me. A few seconds later, she began to giggle. As much as I did not want to laugh, I felt my lips begin to move upward. I joined my sister in laughter. Tears streamed down our cheeks as we allowed the joy and silliness of the moment to fill our soul. Once Lydia composed herself, she wrapped her arms around me and held me tight. Kissing my forehead, she grasped my cheeks. "Come, Sister, I will help so you can get done quicker, and we can get to bed. I will not have us having dark circles under our eyes tomorrow on my wedding day.

Lydia and I worked together pulling the metal tub from the doorway to the front of the crackling fire. I gathered the spices I had to bathe with while Lydia heated the water and poured the steaming liquid into the metal bath. After I bathed, Lydia and I sat in front of the fire as she brushed my hair. I pulled my knees up to my chest and rested my chin on my knees.

"How are you faring, Lydia? Are you anxious about tomorrow?"

I could hear the smile in my sister's voice as she spoke. "Nay, little sister. I am not anxious. I am ready for this next, natural season of my life. I love Matthew, and I am ready to cleave to him."

"I can tell you are happy. And that makes me happy for you, Lydia."

"Thank you, Hadassah. You cannot know how much that means to my heart coming from you. You are growing into a beautiful young woman."

"Well, marriage is still not something I am excited about. But I am trying to accept it. I am sure I will still have my moments of rebellious thoughts, though."

Lydia chuckled. "Your honesty is one of my favorite qualities of yours. But when those feelings come into your soul, always remember we have a father who values love and tenderness over duty and obligation."

"True. And I believe that is the only reason I am willing to work through my feelings."

"I am proud of you, Sister. I have no doubt you will be able to transition into marriage and motherhood beautifully when the time comes," Lydia said as she laid the brush down. "Well, your hair is brushed for now. Tomorrow you will wake up to a mass of unruly, curly hair."

My heart dropped in sadness as Lydia wrapped her arms around me and rested her chin on my shoulder. "Thank you for waking me up, Hadassah. I will cherish this time we had forever."

Tears came and cascaded down my cheeks. "Me too."

Lydia rose slowly and gave me her hands to pull me up. "Come on, little sister. Let's savor our last night as children."

Lydia put her arm around me and pulled me close as we walked to our room. "I cannot believe we did not wake Mama and Papa."

"Me either! They must be weary."

"Should we tell them we heard every word?" Rachel whispered.

Samuel smiled. "No, my love. That will diminish the specialness. Let's just hold this precious moment. It will make it sweeter."

Rachel snuggled up to her husband and laid her head on his chest. She needed his closeness to comfort the breaking of her heart. "You are right, Samuel."

Samuel kissed Rachel's head. "Let us try to get some sleep. Tomorrow will take all our strength to get through."

CHAPTER 12

The next day, I watched Lydia pledge love to her husband before God, her family, and her village. Living as the only child in the house was not something I was used to, and I did not particularly enjoy it. But still, I was determined to enjoy this rare time with my parents. Almost two months later, my family traveled back to Jerusalem for the Festival of Shavot. Time, routine, and the seasons of life unfolded smoothly as they did the year before. Spring and summer faded away, and fall settled in on the rolling hills of Bethlehem.

I woke up to the brilliant pink and orange hues of the sunrise and stretched. I laid for a second, enjoying the warmth and comfort of my bed. A slow smile formed on my lips as I remembered what day it was.

It was my birthday.

I could not believe I was twelve today. How could time feel like it will never move forward, yet in the same moment make me feel rushed, helpless to stop the inevitable passage of growing up? Haste nuzzled my cheek, and I hugged my beloved lamb, thankful he shifted my solemn reverie.

"Good morning, Haste. Can you believe I'm twelve today? One more year with the flock before I become betrothed. I sat up and pulled Haste close, feeling safe in the warmth and softness of the animal. "Do you think I will make a good wife?"

Haste bleated, and I couldn't help but chuckle. A question merits a response, does it not? "Thank you. I know you believe in me. Come on, little lamb. Let's get ready for the day."

I scurried around my half of the room. A curtain separated my space from my parents' room. I did not hear them moving around preparing for the day, which was unusual.

I walked into the small main room with Haste not far behind, and there stood my parents. Putting my hands on my hips, I smiled. "What are you two conspiring?"

"Well, it is not every day our youngest daughter turns twelve."

"Your daughter is an old woman today."

Mama playfully wagged her finger at me. "But never too old for me to put over my knee if I need to."

I offered my mother a cheeky grin. "No, never that."

Papa stepped forward. "Hadassah, your mother and I got you a gift." He pulled the object he had been hiding behind his back.

I gasped—what he held could not have been more perfect. "A new staff! Look, Haste. Oh, Mama, Papa, thank you. It is beautiful!"

My parents beamed in delight at my excitement.

"You're welcome. Andrew made it. I think he did an excellent job." Papa shared.

"That he did. I'll have to thank him when I see him."

"Yes, you will." Papa put his hands on my shoulders and looked in my eyes that were as black as a moonless night.

"Now, Daughter, besides your mother, I know you better than anyone else." Papa glanced at Mama, her eyebrows lifted in question. I had no time to ponder what her expression meant because Papa continued with his lament.

"And I am sure the thought has crossed your mind that in a year, your days with the flock will be over."

I nodded, my eyes serious and solemn.

"I thought this would be your foremost thoughts today. Your mother and I chose a new staff as your gift for this reason. We want your staff to be a reminder to you to live in joy this year. Do not dwell on this being your last year, but have fun, work hard, and be the best shepherd to your flock that you can be."

I hugged my father. "Thank you, Papa."

"You are welcome. Now, go ahead, I will be along in a minute."

"Yes, Papa. Let us go, Haste." I left home with my little companion on my heels, very much unaware of the conversation that was taking place between the two people responsible for my existence.

Samuel turned toward his wife. "What did that look mean?"

Rachel put her hand on her husband's cheek with tenderness. "My love, we do know our daughter very well, but it was Andrew who shared his idea of making Hadassah a staff for her final year."

Samuel blinked. "So?"

Rachael sighed. "Do you not find that rather ... unusual for Andrew?"

Samuel waved his hand. "Nonsense. He would have done the same for our other daughters." He kissed his

Rachel's forehead. "I must be on my way."

Rachel watched her husband leave the house, wondering when he would see the obvious.

CHAPTER 13

"How's the sheepfold coming, Hadassah?" Papa asked.

I wiped the sweat from my face. "Good. I cannot believe how dirty it has gotten, but when I'm finished with it, it will keep the flock warm for the winter."

Papa gave me a knowing look. "Hadassah, you know as well as I do it will be used before winter."

My lungs exhaled, long and slow. "I am trying to forget about it."

"Hadassah, I am leaving in three days."

"I know. You do this every year. But Papa ..." I pointed to the sheep grazing about in the green pasture. "That is my flock, and I love them! The rams being in this sheepfold only reminds me of why they are going to Jerusalem."

Papa's eyes were mixed with compassion and sternness. "Hadassah, Yahweh's ways are higher than our ways. I do not always understand why he asks us to do certain things, but we have to give to God the things we do understand as well as the things we do not understand."

Against my will, my eyes filled with tears. "It is so difficult, Papa. I know you are right, but my heart fills with frustration and anger when I hear this. It is how you always answer, and you say those words so calmly, never faltering or wavering. It is maddening!"

Papa held out his arm. "Come here." I allowed myself to be pulled into my father's embrace. "What you see, my child, is the wisdom from harsh and painful lessons in my youth. I have not always been accepting of God's ways. I, too, have questioned them during different seasons of my life. Do you know what changed my heart?"

I shook my head. "I do not know, Papa."

"God never changed. I may change. My circumstances may change. But God was and is always who he said he would be. I never had to wonder if he would keep his promises, because he always did. If God was constant, then I could trust his ways even if I did not understand them. You see, my love, God does not expect us to be perfect. He only asks us to admit when we need to change and be willing to be set apart. Then he will always give us the strength and grace to do what is right."

I pondered my father's words in the comfort of his embrace. "What do you struggle with, Papa?"

Papa arms dropped his arm and lowered his head.

"Papa, what is it?"

"I have never told you this. But the night Haste was born and you begged me to let him live, I seethed with anger that God led me to honor your request and let Haste live."

I gasped and took a step away from the man I adored. My hand went to my chest in shock. "What? Why, Papa?"

"In all my years of shepherding, I have seen many lambs like Haste. And those lambs did not survive. In my mind, Haste would die within minutes of being born. I believed it would be best to put him out of his misery and avoid the shame of sanctification. You loved him from the moment you saw him, believing he had a purpose. In those moments, God spoke to my heart and told me to listen to my daughter, because he was speaking through you."

His words confused my troubled heart. "If you knew God was saying that, then why were you angered?"

"Because all I believed was what I could see. You loved Haste so much, and I did not want to see you get hurt. It would have pained me to see your heart shattered with this loss. I thought it would be best to proceed with what seemed inevitable so you would not become more attached, causing you an abundance of pain. Even though God told me to listen to you, I did not understand how it would work. The next morning, I knew what God had told me was correct. I do not know why Haste lived. I do not know why he is still here. But I now trust what you have prophesied from the beginning—through a maimed lamb, God has a purpose."

My shoulders slumped at my father's confession. My body trembled with every kind of emotion not knowing which one to settle on. "I do not know what to say, Papa. You were supportive of me. I could sense your urgency the night Haste was born, but I never felt anger from you."

Papa took my hand with tender care. "Mamas and papas love their children so much that even when we do not see how something our children desperately desires will work, we know dismissing their dreams will hurt them more than it will help. So, we are their comfort when it does not work, and when it seems the impossible happens, we are also there to celebrate."

I smiled at my father's beautiful description of a parent's unconditional love. "I love you, Papa. Thank you for celebrating with me."

Papa squeezed my hand. "Oh, Daughter, you do not even know how much I love you."

My lips split into a crooked grin as I looked up at my father. "I did not know twelve would bring so much wisdom."

Papa laughed. “Just wait until you turn thirteen.”

My heart sank at those words, but I managed to smile. I held my hand up. “Papa, one life lesson at a time.”

Papa looked into my eyes. I wondered if he saw how they were mixed with sadness and acceptance of what my thirteenth year would bring. But I hoped they also held a maturity and will to trust God with the things I did not understand. If he saw these things, as I suspected he did, I hoped a burden lifted from his heart in seeing that his daughter would cross the threshold of womanhood with grace, strength, and dignity.

Papa and I gathered all the male lambs that were born during lambing season. Fifty-six first-born rams had entered our flock this season and that number was about to diminish.

“All right, Hadassah, I will count off, and every eighth ram, please take to the sheepfold.”

“Yes, Papa.”

Papa took his staff and began counting and tapping lambs. “One ... four ... eight.”

I picked up the first lamb, took it to the sheepfold, and secured the gate. I walked back to my father and the other rams. Papa’s eyes were glazed with emotion as he pointed to the structure. “Look at Haste.”

I turned and saw my pet lamb nuzzling the young ram’s head. My eyes filled with tears at the precious and profound sight. “It is as if is he knows why that ram is in there.”

Papa nodded, his eyes reflecting the wonderment he felt. “I think he knows. I believe we are witnessing a small portion of what Haste’s purpose is.”

CHAPTER 14

Mama put her hands on her hips. “I do not like that your father gave you permission to be with the flock this week.”

I smiled. “But Mama, he explained why. This is my last year with the flock, so he wants me to have every minute with them that I can.”

“I realize that, but to walk there and back home by yourself is not proper for a woman, especially a young unwed woman.”

“That is why he said I had to wait until eight. Now it is completely daylight, and it is just a short walk to the pasture.”

“Anything could happen in ten minutes.”

I sighed. This had been our main conversation ever since Papa left, and I was growing weary of it. “Mama, nothing is going to happen. Besides, I have Haste with me.”

Mama rolled her eyes and threw her hands in the air in defeat. “Oh, LORD, what am I going to do with this strong-willed child?”

“I'm sure the LORD will help you think of something,” I said dryly.

I grabbed my staff and placed my hand on the door handle when a sudden knock startled both Mama and me. “Who is it?” I asked.

"It is Andrew."

I opened the door to see the tall shepherd standing on the other side. "Good morning, Andrew. I was just about to come to work."

"I thought so. I left Julius with the flock so I could come and escort you to the fold. I will walk you back to your house at noon as well."

I paused. Andrew was a kind man, but his thoughtfulness of me was a surprise. It also touched me, causing my heart to feel things it never had before, things I wasn't sure I was ready for. "Oh. Well, thank you," I said, finally finding my voice. I looked at Mama and raised my eyebrow "The Lord works in mysterious ways."

Mama smiled smugly. "Thank you, Andrew."

Shaking my head in good humor, I kissed Mama goodbye. "I'll see you at noon. Let's go, Haste."

For the first few minutes, Andrew and I walked in silence. The awkwardness was maddening. I had to say something. "Did I ever thank you for the staff?"

Andrew smiled. "You have many times."

"Oh. Well, thank you again."

"You are welcome. Do you think your father and Jonathan made it to Jerusalem yet?"

"Oh, I am sure. Papa likes to leave camp at first light before it gets too hot."

"That is wise."

I studied Andrew's sharp jaw line. "Why did you not go this year?"

"It was Jonathan's turn," Andrew said simply. I did not know him well enough to push for an explanation, but I knew there was more to his not going than that.

"I see. How is your carpentry business faring?"

"Very well. I am working on a table right now."

"Are you close to finishing it? I am sorry you will not be able to tend to your carpentry work this week."

Andrew smiled. "Oh, do not be sorry. I love being with the sheep in the pasture. It is the most peaceful place to be."

"I think so too," I said softly.

We smiled at each together and walked the rest of the way in content silence.

The rest of the week developed into somewhat of a routine. Andrew would walk me to the pasture and then back to my house for the noonday meal. During that week, Andrew and I found we worked very well together. I appreciated the way Andrew tenderly took care of the sheep. Haste even willingly went with Andrew, when usually I had to order him to go with another person—even Papa. We formed a sweet familiarity with each other, and I cherished the wonderful friend Andrew came to be to me.

On Andrew's part, he could not believe how a woman could be so self-sufficient and confident, and yet so unassuming. He could not imagine a more beautiful woman with an equally beautiful heart. And during that week, he came to love the young Jewish woman even more.

CHAPTER 15

"Daughter, hurry! The sheep are waiting."

I came out of my room, laughing at my father's impatience. "It is always the same each year the week you return from Jerusalem. You are so eager to get back to the flock," I said as I braided my unruly curly black hair.

"I know, and I do not know why. It is not like this when we return from Jerusalem after festivals."

"Well, you are surrounded by family that you do not see day after day. And I am sure the distraction of grandchildren can make a man forget he is a shepherd and has a flock."

Papa's joyful laugh filled the tiny home. "What you say is true. Are you ready?"

"Yes, Papa."

"Andrew, Jonathan, good morning!" Papa greeted his hirelings.

"Good morning, sir."

"Yes, good morning, sir. It is good to have you back." Andrew said shaking his employer's hand.

"Thank you! It is good to be back."

Andrew turned to me and smiled. "Good morning."

My heartbeat in a unrhythmic fashion, and I felt my cheeks flush with heat. "Good morning. I missed my escort this morning."

"And I missed escorting you."

Papa looked from Andrew to me. "What are you speaking of?"

"Papa, last week while you were away, Andrew was very kind. He escorted me to the flock each morning and then back home for the noonday meal."

"But I did not tell him to," Papa told me as if Andrew was not there.

I looked at Andrew, my eyes begging him to give an explanation. "I know, sir. But since this was the first time Hadassah came to the flock while you were in Jerusalem, I wanted to be cautious."

Papa faced Andrew, his eyes burning into the young Jewish man. "I *was* being cautious. That was why she was not to leave our home until eight each morning. Do you actually believe you care more about my daughter's care and safety than I?"

I stared at Papa for several seconds. Where did my good natured, practical father go? "Papa," I said softly, "No one is faulting the arrangements you set for me. Andrew was just doing what he knew you would do in this situation. Mama was very appreciative. I am not sure why you are not."

Papa frowned. "I am sorry. Thank you for keeping Hadassah safe." His clipped tone revealed his true feelings—he was anything but sorry.

We watched the two hirelings walk away in uncomfortable silence.

"Let's get to work," Papa said with a flat tone, without looking at me.

I walked calmly behind my father. I knew what his tone meant. No discussion of what just transpired was to be broached. But inside I was seething and telling Papa exactly what I thought of his cruel and embarrassing actions towards his hireling.

The walk from the sheep pasture to our cabin was suffocating with the loudest silence I have ever experienced. Papa and I entered our small home to partake of the noonday meal. I was relieved to have Mama present—the only person who could make Papa see reason.

"Go retrieve some water, Hadassah."

Mama turned to Papa. "But we have plenty of water."

"Go, Hadassah."

I grabbed the pitcher and walked out of the house, Haste following close behind.

"Samuel, what is troubling you?"

"Why did you not inform me that Andrew escorted Hadassah to the flock while I was gone?"

"Samuel, you did not return from your journey until late last night. Then, you left at dawn this morning. There has been no time for me to share with you how we fared last week while you were in Jerusalem. But why does it seem as if Andrew's care for our daughter bothers you?"

Samuel proudly put his hand to his chest. "*I* had everything under control. Andrew did not need to interfere. I do not like that this pious Jewish youth acts as if he can take better care of my daughter than I can."

Rachel's chuckle contrasted with her husband's tirade. "This attentiveness is far more than caring."

Samuel blinked. "What do you mean?"

Rachel tenderly touched his cheek. "Andrew is in love with our daughter."

Samuel pushed Rachel's hand away. "That is absurd! What makes you think that?"

Rachel bit her lip to keep from laughing. She had never seen her husband jealous. It was as endearing as it was ridiculous. "My love, look at the past two years. He made us new eating tools, he created Hadassah a beautiful staff with intricate details, he volunteered to stay with the flock while you and Jonathan went to Jerusalem, and he escorted our daughter to and from the pasture every day you were away."

Samuel frowned and crossed his arms. "He's too old for her," he muttered.

"Samuel, there is eleven years between them. Might I remind you there is a sixteen-year age difference between us and an eight-to-ten-year age difference between our other daughters and their husbands. You will sound like a fool if you say age difference is why you disapprove."

Samuel leaned on the brick wall. "I have been thinking of letting Hadassah remain here with the flock another year."

Rachel's eyes narrowed. "When did you begin thinking this?"

"Last week while I was gone."

Rachel sighed and rubbed her temples. "I knew this would happen."

"What?"

"Samuel, you are not a normal Jewish man. You treat me and our daughters with utmost care and respect. We are more than child bearers to you. You deeply love your daughters, and people are in awe of how happy you are even though you have no sons. Most men would feel shame and resent their wives."

"I do not know what you are trying to say to me."

"You have always had a special place in your heart for Hadassah. She is your baby, and she has always had the same love for our flock that you do. You have always held on a little tighter to Hadassah. Letting go of her is not going to be an easy feat for you."

Tears filled Samuel's eyes, his true tender character coming to light. "I do not want to lose my girl."

Rachel wiped her husband's tears and hugged Samuel. "I know. But she is not a girl anymore. She is a woman. A woman who is ready for a husband, a family—a woman quite capable of running her household. Waiting another year will not help. Andrew will wait for Hadassah as long as he needs to—of that I am certain. You have to let our daughter go, and who better to let her go to than Andrew? A man who will love and cherish her just like her Papa has."

Samuel's response was to kiss Rachel on her cheek and then her lips. He proceeded to put the bread and cheese on the table, and Rachel knew she had said enough. She knew her husband very well, and she had no doubt her youngest would be betrothed in a year—and she had no doubt who her betrothed would be.

Samuel wiped his face. "Andrew, Jonathan, I am leaving for the night."

"Very well, sir. Have a good night," Jonathan said.

Samuel looked at Andrew. "Could I speak to you, please?"

The two men walked away a bit for privacy. Samuel looked at Andrew. "Do you love my daughter?"

Not breaking eye contact, Andrew answered. "Yes, very much."

Samuel shook his head. "I ask for your forgiveness for my words this morning ... it is just that she is my last one, and—"

Andrew cut Samuel off. "I understand, sir, and I forgive you."

Samuel looked straight ahead for a few seconds. "You may have my daughter's hand if you wish," he said in a near whisper, but Andrew heard what the older man had said.

"I would consider it the highest honor that has ever been bestowed on me to have your daughter as my wife, sir."

Samuel looked away. He knew he was doing the right thing, but it did not stop his heart from feeling like it would burst in pain. "I would still ask some things of you."

"You are her father, sir. I will proceed in whatever manner you wish."

"I thank you. First, even though I have chosen you to wed my daughter, I still want to wait for the betrothal until she is thirteen. She has barely crossed the threshold of being a girl to becoming a woman and I'd like her to have some time to adjust. In accordance with this, I would ask you to keep this news between us. I will tell my wife, of course, but I want Hadassah to enjoy her last year completely. I worry if she knows you are her intended, she will be nervous and distracted."

"I agree, sir. I know how much she loves her sheep, and I want this last year to be one of her most cherished memories."

"I have one more request. This time, you are free to say no, but I know this would make Hadassah happy."

"What is it?"

"Would you consider allowing Hadassah to keep Haste after you are married?"

Andrew smiled. "I would not dream of separating them."

Samuel broke into a joyous smile, and he clapped Andrew on the back. "Very good. Welcome to the family."

"Thank you, sir!"

"Good night."

"Good night, sir."

Andrew was awed as he watched his future father-in-law walk away. After this morning, he believed he would be dismissed and never offered Hadassah's hand. The days and months were sure to go by slowly, but in a year, they would be betrothed, and then in two years he would have the woman he had loved for years as his wife.

I pulled my heavy animal skin coat tighter around me. The rain was pouring in sheets as it did this time of December, but the milking still had to be done. The sheep bleated in agitation. I patted the animal to comfort. "Easy, I am almost done."

I squirted the milk into the goat skin until it reached the rim. "Finished. Now, go to Papa."

The ewe ran to the sheepfold, and Papa was there to dry her off. I milked two more sheep, then ran with the last ewe to the warm structure. I threw the skin coat off and squeezed the water from my hair. "Mama did a fine job with this coat. It has kept me very warm and dry."

"I am sorry they do not allow me to milk them anymore. They just prefer your gentle touch over my rough, calloused hands."

I sat down in the warm straw, and Haste laid his head on my lap. "It is a mystery to me how my hands are still soft and smooth with all the work I do with the flock."

I said, looking at my small hands and perfectly round fingernails. "'Tis no worry, Papa. You know I do not mind."

Papa shook his head. "I still cannot believe you have to make Haste go with me when he needs to. He would have stayed by your side in the rain if you had not ordered him to the sheepfold."

I caressed Haste's head. "Did I tell you that whenever Andrew called for him when you were gone, Haste went to him straight away? Andrew has become a dear friend. I will miss his presence when I become betrothed," I said softly, still unsure of the feelings that man stirred within my heart,

"No, you did not tell me, but that is good." Papa did not elaborate, but he had apologized to me for his actions toward Andrew.

Samuel looked at Haste and shook his head. *How could that lamb be so perceptive? One might believe he was dim-witted because of his maimed leg and his small size for his age, but so far, he has defeated the odds by surviving a dangerous birth, he comforted a sacrificial lamb as if he knew its fate, and he sensed Andrew was significant in his life somehow.* It had taken Samuel several years to see the truth, but he now knew—Haste was one special lamb.

I worked over the loom as Mama kneaded the dough. Weaving was not a skill I came to as easily as my sisters, but I was determined to master it. As I wove, my mind wandered to my upcoming betrothment. In ten months, I would be promised to a man. I did not know who he would be, but as custom dictated, Papa would take care of all the arrangements for me. With each passing day, my heart accepted I would be getting married and leaving my flock. After the talk I had with my father, I worked on committing my fears and doubts to God. When I did this, it was just as Papa said, God gave me grace and strength. Still the transition from being a part of a shepherd family to supporting whatever profession my husband performed worried me.

"Mama?"

"Yes, love?"

"When you married Papa was it strange going from being the daughter of an innkeeper to being the wife of a shepherd?"

Mama chuckled. "Very. Your love for your flock was the same kind of love I had for my papa's inn. The busyness of it, meeting new people and hearing their stories—every day was an adventure. Moving from the crowded city of Bethlehem to its quiet hills was quite a change."

"Did you hate it?"

Mama tilted her head to the side. "I did not hate it, but I did have to adapt. Your father's attentiveness and care helped me, and within a few months, I became pregnant with Miriam, and that became my life. I would never trade your father, you, or your sisters for five hundred inns."

I smiled. "I am happy to hear that. But I do not think Grandfather would say the same thing."

Mama grinned. "He does love the inn, but shall I tell you a secret?"

"Yes, please."

"His favorite place is the stable cave."

"He told me that!"

Mama's eyes became wide. "He did? That is a secret he tries to hide. But he holds a special place in his heart for you. You look so much like my mama—even more than I do. I am sure Papa feels like he is looking at her when he looks at you. Ever since I was a little girl, he has been drawn to that cave. The drawing became stronger after Mama died. After the dining hall was clean and the guests were asleep, Papa would go to the cave to get away from the inn and talk to God. To him it is the most peaceful place he can be."

"I could sense that when he told me. He shared with me that if he had never married or had children, he would have nothing to talk to God about when he went to the cave each night."

Mama shook her head. "I always believed God had a special purpose for that cave."

I smiled softly. "The cave is grandfather's Haste."

Mama tilted her head to the side, amazed at the revelation. "I believe you are right, Hadassah. The cave is Papa's Haste.

The cold, rainy days of January passed slowly as they usually did. Finally, at the end of February, it appeared the rains were behind us. The last day in February, Papa announced it was time to get the lambs sheared before lambing season began.

Papa, Andrew, and I stood in the pasture watching the sheep graze. They had been watered, fed, milked, and now it was time to make the trek into the city for shearing, which would take all four shepherds.

Other shepherds wondered why we didn't shear our sheep. Why would we pay someone else to provide this service? I loved how Papa responded, "So many of my neighbors have supported me so I could put food on my family's table, and I desire to show others that kindness."

"Hadassah, would you like to do the honors?"

I smiled. This was one of my favorite tasks to do as a shepherd. "I would love to." I cupped my hands around my mouth and shouted. "Tahoo! Tahoo!"

The sheep came over to me and waited to follow my lead. "Hadassah and Andrew, you lead, and Jonathan and I will follow behind the flock," said Papa.

We made the twenty-minute walk to the marketplace. Thankfully, no other shepherds were using the shearer's services. I was always amazed how our sheep patiently stood as the shearer straddled the animal. It was as if they knew their shepherds were doing what was best for them. Excess wool would only burden them. With quick efficiency, the shearer cut the wool, Papa sold the wool, and we were back in the pasture with the sheep in two hours.

While the sheep grazed, I just watched them, feeling at peace. Haste shifted beside me and yawned. I watched as Andrew walked toward me, wiping the sweat from his brow. My stomach swirled around like David's sling, a feeling that was becoming familiar whenever I was around the man.

"Hello," he said as he sat down.

"Hello. You can leave if you need to, Andrew. We do not want to keep you from your carpentry business."

"No, you are not keeping me. I enjoy sitting and watching the sheep after a hard day of work. Besides, in a few months, I will begin carpentry full-time."

I stared at him in surprise. "Oh," I said softly. "I will miss you, but I am happy for you."

Andrew smiled. "Thank you. I asked your father that I be the one to tell you. I bought a plot of land in the city. Soon I will begin building a home that will house my carpentry business." I could tell there was so much more he wanted to say, but he hid those words in his heart.

I nodded. I chastised my stomach for the twisting it did whenever Andrew was close to me. A man with his demeanor was surely either betrothed or pursuing a woman who he wished would become his wife. I do not know why, but my heart clinched in pain thinking of Andrew with another woman. "You will be busy. But your work is beautiful. It will suit you well."

"Thank you."

We fell into a comfortable silence, enjoying each other's presence. Over the last year, we had developed a sweet friendship.

"When I came to sit beside you, you looked lost in thought. Is something troubling you?"

"I would not say troubling, but I do feel a stirring in my soul. Have you ever had a restlessness in your spirit? A restlessness that tells you something profound and divine is about to happen?"

Andrew shook his head. "I do not believe I have."

I looked at the animal lying beside me. "I have felt that with Haste at times—when he was born and when he comforted the sacrificial lamb. But this feeling does not have to do with Haste. I believe amazing things are happening right now that I would not be able to believe or comprehend."

I looked at Andrew and shook my head. "I know I must sound mad."

"I do not believe you are mad. I have known you a long time, and I know how spiritually intuitive you are. I do not know what your urgency is leading you to, but I know Yahweh will reveal it to you in due time."

CHAPTER 16:

Lambing season, Passover, Shavout, and spring passed uncharacteristically fast for all of us who lived in Bethlehem. I saw very little of Andrew, and that saddened me, but I cherished the time I had with the flock. September came upon Bethlehem, which was known for its intense heat, but to me, it was my last month as a single woman.

I walked out of my room and saw, as usual, Papa waiting for Haste and me. Papa smiled. “I am going to miss this next month.”

“Me too. It will be a different season of life, but I am sure I will enjoy that year with Mama.”

“She is looking at the time with joy. She tries not to show it because she knows you will be sad, but October twentieth can’t come soon enough for her.”

I giggled at the thought of my transparent mother trying to hide her excitement. “One thing Mama has never been is discreet.” My fingers effortlessly formed my hair into a braid. “Do you think it will be hot?”

“Very. We must bring plenty of water today.”

Despite the heat, Papa and I worked very hard and came home famished. After the noonday meal, I went to work on my loom. I was working on a rug for the new home I would share with a husband. I knew that time was a year away, but weaving was not something I excelled at, and I wanted all of the practice I could get.

A few hours later, Papa walked through the door.

"Samuel, you are home early."

"I know, my love, but I have some news."

Mama and I took in Papa's seriousness. "What is it, Papa?"

"Jonathan and I were visited by Roman soldiers today. Caesar Augustus has ordered the whole world to be taxed. Every man must return to the place of his birth with his family to be counted and taxed."

Mama put her hand to her cheek. Nothing of this political magnitude had ever happened. "But why?"

Papa shook his head. "I do not know. But with most men in power, it usually stems from greed."

"When will this take place?" I asked.

"Everyone has a month to report."

Mama's sigh revealed her weariness. "I am so thankful all of our family and friends were born in Bethlehem."

Papa shook his head in agreement. "I pity the man who will have to travel for this ridiculous decree."

The next month passed quickly, despite my attempts to slow it down, but it was the most rewarding time I ever had with the flock.

The morning before my thirteenth birthday, I rolled over, stretched, and looked at my beloved lamb. "Come here, Haste."

The animal happily climbed in my lap, and I rested my chin on Haste's head. Had Haste been born with no complications or deformities, he would have been too big for me to hold, but his weakness gave me strength. My little companion would always be small enough for me to hold. "This is it, Haste. My last day with the flock. After today, I will not be the family shepherd anymore. I will be betrothed. So many changes. I hope I will make everyone proud."

I proceeded to get ready for the day and then walked out to the living room. I stopped, stunned to see Papa leaning on the doorpost with tears streaming down his face.

Tears filled my eyes at the sight of my tender-hearted father weeping. "Oh, Papa."

Papa took me in his arms. "No man is prouder of his daughter than I am. Ten sons could never give me the joy you have."

I tried to contain my sobs. "I love you, Papa."

Papa kissed my forehead. "I love you too. Come now, the flock awaits."

Throughout the day, I performed my daily tasks for the last time. For the past seven years, this flock had been my life. Now my normal was about to change. The sheep even acted sad, as if they knew this day was significant somehow.

After the sheep were watered and milked, I sat down and enjoyed the breeze, loving the fragrance of flowers it brought. Papa finished his task of checking the sheep for blemishes and then sat next to me. "How are you faring today?"

"I am sad, but I have determined in my heart to look at this new season in my life as a grand adventure."

Papa smiled. "Like your dreams?"

I grinned at my father. "Yes, like my dreams. I may never take passage on a merchant ship to Persia to deliver goods or play my flute for the queen of Egypt, but being the family shepherd of this flock will always be one of the best things I have accomplished in my life."

The corners of Papa's lips lifted into a sad smile. "I remember the first time I brought you to the flock."

"I was so excited. I had waited for that day for so long."

"Lydia as well. She could not wait until you were old enough to fill the job of family shepherd."

I giggled, remembering my sister's dramatics. "Very true."

"The first day, you were most excited to milk the ewes, but your little hands could not master it. It broke my heart when tears filled your big black eyes."

With that memory, tears flooded my eyes just as they did seven years ago.

Papa put his hand over his chest with pomp. "It still breaks my heart."

I smiled and wiped the tears off my cheeks. "Papa, may I ask you something?"

"Of course."

"I have never done this before, but I would love very much to sleep with my flock tonight."

Papa squeezed my shoulder, and I could see the love and adoration he had for me in his eyes. "We will go first thing after the evening meal."

We sat in comfortable silence watching the flock. "The sheep seem sad."

"I had the same thought."

"I know what would give them cheer."

I grinned and took my flute out of my receptacle. Then, just as I did when I was a little girl, I danced and played a cheerful tune, and one last time the sheep danced in delight with me—their shepherd.

CHAPTER 17

Samuel, Andrew, and Jonathan sat on the hillside watching Hadassah sit among the sheep, talking and singing to them.

"I do not think she will ever forget this night." Samuel said.

Andrew smiled as his eyes danced with love. "I agree, sir. Having her as my wife will be nothing short of an adventure."

"That reminds me. Tomorrow, allow me and Hadassah to have some time so I can prepare her for the betrothal ceremony."

"Yes, sir."

"Jonathan, will you fare all right with the flock by yourself for about an hour?"

"Of course, sir."

"Very good." Samuel turned to call out to his daughter. "Hadassah! Come over here with us now."

I walked over to the men and fell on the grass with no grace and in good humor. "I do not know why we have never slept under the stars with the flock before, Papa. It is invigorating!"

Papa laughed and stole a glance at Andrew, who was grinning like a foolish child. "It is exciting. I am happy we were able to do this. Are you ready to get some sleep?"

I was glad Papa and Andrew made amends, and I was glad Papa invited Andrew to spend this very special night with us, but what I just witnessed between them seemed peculiar to me. "Oh, Papa, I could not sleep now."

"I figured as much. Well, why not ready the bedrolls so when we are ready to rest, they will be there."

I jumped up. "That is a good thought, Papa. I will—"

Suddenly, the night sky flooded with light. I looked up, and what I saw made my breath catch in my throat. The heavens were split open, and a man dressed all in white, outshined the stars and the moon.

The men stood up with me, and I grabbed my father's arm. "Papa, what is happening?"

"I do not know," he said breathlessly.

"Fear not!" The man's voice echoed in the sky. "For behold, I bring you good tidings of great joy, which will be to all people. For unto you is born this day in the city of David, a Savior, which is Christ the Lord."

We looked at each other in awe as the angel continued. "And this shall be a sign unto you; ye shall find the babe wrapped in swaddling clothes, lying in a manger."

Out of thin air, thousands of like beings appeared with the angel, illuminating the sky. I gasped as they burst into the most beautiful singing I had ever heard. "Glory to God in the highest, and on earth peace, good will toward men."

As quickly as they appeared, they vanished. Andrew broke the stunned silence first. "Did that just happen?"

I clasped my hands together in joy. "Oh, can you believe it? The Messiah has come."

Papa smiled, "Let's go find him."

My eyes lit up in surprise and yearning. "Oh, Papa, can

we?"

"I think we are supposed to. Those angels would never have appeared and told us where to find him if we were not supposed to."

"What will we do with the flock?" Jonathan asked.

"We will put them in the sheepfold. After what we just witnessed, we know Yahweh will shield them from danger. Hadassah, Haste must go into the sheepfold as well. We must act quickly, and he will slow us down."

We put the sheep in the sheepfold and turned to leave. Haste began bleating and pawing on at the gate. I looked at my father. "We cannot leave him, Papa—he knows."

Papa nodded in the animal's direction. "Go retrieve him, and let us go with haste."

With quick steps, we made it to the city. "Where do you think we will find him?" Andrew asked. "The angel said we would find him wrapped in swaddling clothes, laying in a manger. We know he will not be in an inn, but to my knowledge, I know of no stables that would be a large or suitable enough of a structure to have a woman give birth and provide shelter for a family."

I gasped. A beautiful epiphany bloomed in my heart. "I know where he is." The men followed me, and in a few short minutes, we came upon the most beautiful sight I had ever seen. There, in the stable cave my grandfather owned, was the Savior of the world wrapped in swaddling clothes, lying in a manger with an invisible light illuminating the cave. It was just as the angel had said.

Sitting by the manger was a man and a young woman. I put Haste, who was squirming to be out of my arms, on the ground. "Papa, she is my age!"

The man and woman finally noticed us watching them. The young mother picked up the baby protectively.

Papa stepped forward, and we followed our patriarch. "My apologies for frightening you. I am Samuel, and this is my daughter, Hadassah, and those men are Andrew and Jonathan. This might sound strange, but we were visited by an angel of the Lord, and he told us how to find the Christ child."

The couple smiled at each other. "We are no strangers to angel encounters. I am Joseph, this is my wife, Mary, and this," he said with a tender smile, "this is Jesus."

Slowly, in a reverent awe, I came close to Mary and knelt to get a better look at the baby. Tears filled my eyes. He was perfect. His attentive eyes held mine as if he knew who he was and why I was there. "He is so beautiful," I whispered.

Mary looked at her son and then back at me. "Would you like to hold him?"

"Oh, you just had him. I would not want to take your son from you so soon after he was born."

Mary looked at Joseph and then back at me. "He is not mine. He is for all mankind."

Mary handed Jesus to me. I sat in shock at the privilege that was bestowed on me as I rocked the Savior of the world. Papa, Andrew, and Jonathan gathered around me. All three men had tears streaming down their cheeks. Jesus continued to stare at me until his face crumbled and he began to cry.

"Oh, Jesus," I soothed. "You are okay, little one."

The infant was not comforted. I contemplated giving Jesus back to his mother, until I saw Haste coming toward me. That little lamb dragged his maimed leg behind him, walked to Jesus, and began nuzzling the head of the Messiah in comfort. Jesus's tears ceased, and his little hand emerged from the swaddling clothes to rest on Haste's head. I gasped and watched in awe as Haste's maimed hind leg slowly and beautifully straightened into a healthy and perfectly straight leg without deformity.

Tears streamed down my face as I looked at Papa. Tears were in his eyes as well, and he shook his head in amazement. In that moment, I sensed my father now knew what I knew. Here, a maimed lamb that should not be alive, a lamb who should have atoned for Israel's sin but could not because he was not perfect, was the lamb who comforted the perfect lamb of God—a maimed lamb who was now made perfect because he believed what mortal men could not. What we had just witnessed was an act of love, a miracle ... a divine purpose.

CHAPTER 18

After we left that night, Grandfather spent his time in the cave with the Messiah. According to him, it was the most peaceful night he had ever experienced. We told everyone we could that the Savior had been born. Some believed and their souls filled with the same joy and awe we had in our hearts. Some did not and thought us mad—even the proof of Haste could not persuade them.

When we awoke the next morning, Papa and I made our way home. I could not wait to tell Mama what we encountered.

I swung the door open, "Mama! You will never believe what happened last night. Right as we were preparing for bed the—"

Papa put his hand on my shoulder. "Hadassah, we will tell your mother at the noon meal. Right now, I want you to wash up and put on your best tunic."

"Why, Papa?"

"Because the man I have chosen to be your husband will be here soon to meet you and sign the marriage contract."

I felt as if I had been punched in the gut. I could physically feel the color drain from my cheeks. I grabbed the table with both hands and inhaled and exhaled slowly. Haste began nuzzling my leg, concerned I was hurt.

"Hadassah," Papa's voice the most tender I had ever heard, "Do you trust me? Have I ever put you in harm's way?"

"No, Papa—never."

"Yes, my daughter. When fear threatens to consume you, remind yourself of this truth."

An hour later, I walked into the main house cleaned and refreshed. I sat down on my mat and my faithful companion curled up beside me."

"You look beautiful, Hadassah."

I managed a small smile. "Thank you, Mama."

I can trust Papa, I can trust Papa ...

"Hadassah, did you hear the knock at the door?"

"No, Papa. I was lost in thought—reminding myself I could trust you."

Papa softly chuckled. "Your betrothed is at the door. Go greet him."

If I had been of sound mind, I would have questioned Papa's command. This was not proper according to our Jewish traditions. I slowly rose and walked to the door. I put my hand on the door handle and exhaled. In one quick motion, I opened the door and gasped.

"Hello, Hadassah."

"Andrew! Are you ... are you my betrothed?"

The silliest and most handsome grin appeared on his lips. "Yes, I am your betrothed."

So that was the reason for Andrew and Papa's strange behavior last night. Tears of relief and joy filled my eyes. "I am so happy it is you."

The next year, I remained home with Mama, gaining valuable experience on how to run a Jewish household, and spent time with Andrew so we could get to know each other better before our wedding. A day after I turned fourteen, I married Andrew in front of our family and friends. I'll never forget that day. Mama and my sisters dressed me in beautiful bridal garments and pinned my unruly curly hair up in a beautiful design. At Andrew's request, ringlets were left at my neck and around my face—he so loved my curls. At last, Mama secured my veil that would cover my face, I was ready to meet my beloved. I held Papa's arm proudly as he led me to Andrew. My sisters stood by my side as my bridesmaids, and Andrew's brothers were his groomsmen. My veil covered my face, but my heart leapt for joy as I looked at Andrew's face. Tears were in his eyes, but his smile reflected his joy, peace, and the love he had for me. My eye caught Lydia's smile beaming on her face. The words she spoke to me years ago floated in my soul like a gentle, cool breeze—when my time came, I would be ready to be a wife and ready for all the things that would come with this new title.

After a joyous day of eating the marvelous food Mama prepared and celebrating our union with guests, my husband and I walked hand in hand to our chuppah room. As Andrew secured the door, I walked to the other side of the room, trying to remember how to breathe. I flinched when I felt gentle hands touch my shoulders.

"What troubles you, my love? You are trembling."

"I am frightened," I whispered.

"Hadassah," Andrew said softly. "May I take your veil off so I can see your face?"

I nodded my head. I felt his hands slowly lift my wedding veil off, and with great care, turn me around to face him. I could only imagine my eyes widened with fear across my face. I must have seemed so young and inexperienced to him.

Andrew took my hands in his. “Please, take to heart what I have to say, because I mean these words with all my heart. There is no plan tonight. We do this our way. Let’s sit, talk, and see where the night takes us.”

I exhaled as the burden I had been carrying lifted. “Thank you, Andrew.”

“You’re welcome. And remember something of grave importance. I have never done this before either. We will learn together.”

For the first time since we entered our sacred room, a smile slowly formed on my lips. “I will be forever grateful my father chose you for me.”

Andrew caressed my cheek. “Me too, my love.”

Andrew and I talked for many hours. We shared our hopes and dreams for our marriage, how many children we wanted to have if Yahweh chose to bless and open my womb, and what their names would be, and even how I wanted to set up the cabin Andrew built for us. Then, in the most natural way, my husband took me in his arms, and I felt no dread or trepidation—I felt safe and cherished.

The next morning, our wedding party followed Andrew, Haste, and me to our cabin in the city to partake of a beautiful and bountiful wedding feast. When our guests left our home, relief swept over me. The part I looked forward to the most was upon me—Andrew and I would discover our own rituals, our own customs, and our own convictions as husband and wife in the sight of our God. Our lives were no longer separate. They were one.

Andrew enjoyed being a full-time carpenter, and he was very successful. To our delight, Joseph and Mary decided to make Bethlehem their home. The couple’s cabin was only a few miles from ours, so we saw them often. Andrew was overjoyed when he learned that Joseph was a carpenter too. The two men consulted each other on several pieces they were working on and even partnered on a couple of orders that were extensive.

Mary became a dear friend of mine, and each time I went to the marketplace, I stopped at Mary's cabin to visit and to see Jesus. Every time I saw Jesus, I marveled at who he was. To others he was just a baby, but to me, he was the Son of God. Looking at him, I remembered the night he was born in Grandfather's stable cave.

One day, Mary told me about the night three wisemen appeared at their door. These men had traveled from a far-off land, guided by a star to see the Messiah, so they could worship him. Each man had a gift for Jesus—gold, frankincense, and myrrh. Joseph built a shelf in their small home's main room where the gifts of the wisemen sat. This baby had that effect on everyone—men and women would stop Mary and Joseph in public, asking if they could hold the Christ Child. The tiny baby resonated the hope and yearning the Jewish race felt in their souls. But I was about to see that Jesus's birth would not only bring peace and joy but pain and turmoil as well.

CHAPTER 19

Andrew and I could not wait to have a baby. Most women became with child a few months after being married, but it took me a whole year to conceive. Andrew was thrilled and began making a cradle as soon as I told him I was to have a baby. Haste followed me around everywhere, as if to make sure the baby and I were faring well. It was the most amazing experience to feel my baby growing inside of me.

By my eighth month, my waist had expanded so far that attending to my daily duties became difficult. By evening, all I could do was sit and rest as Andrew read from the Law. One such night, Andrew had just began reading the Torah. Haste was lying beside me, and with Andrew's steady deep voice soothing my weary soul, I began to drift to sleep. Suddenly, the door was kicked open, and Roman soldiers barged in our home. Andrew and I stood in shock.

"Can I help you?" Andrew asked, not hiding the anger from his voice.

The Roman soldiers ignored my husband, and the soldier in charge looked at me with his evil, steely eyes. "Search the place," he ordered.

The three other soldiers searched every corner of our home. I flinched as I heard dishes break and furniture thrown to the ground.

"There are no baby boys here, sir," one of the soldiers reported to his superior.

The head soldier smirked. He placed the tip of his sword on my stomach, glaring at Andrew as if daring him to do something. Andrew's mouth twitched, but he remained unwavering, knowing anything he did would result in my death as well as that of our unborn baby. "You better thank the gods that baby is still inside you," he sneered.

As soon as the soldiers left, Andrew caught me as my knees buckled. "Why were they searching for baby boys? And why did it sound like they wanted to kill them? What about my nephews? Oh, my nephews!" I sobbed.

"Shh," Andrew soothed. "Hadassah, do not assume the worst."

"I need to go to Mama and Papa's."

"No, not this late. And not in your condition."

"Andrew, please. If something has happened with my nephews, I need to be there. I need to be there for my sisters."

Andrew sighed. "Very well, my love."

Andrew and I began our journey to my parents' home. The sky echoed with screams and moans—it was just as I had always imagined the days of Moses had been when every first born was killed by the angel of death.

I will never forget the sight I witnessed when I walked into my childhood home. There sat all four of my sisters with their families, sobbing. My brothers-in-law's expressions were ashen as they stared into space with the most hopeless looks I had ever seen.

Papa came to me and pulled me into a tender and sad embrace. "We are so thankful you are well, daughter."

"Why, Papa, why?"

"It would seem King Herod ordered every baby boy two years and younger to be killed. As for why, no one knows."

"So that means ..."

Papa's eyes filled with tears. "Yes. Isaac, Asher, Adam, Caleb, Daniel, and Elijah are all with God now."

"Oh, dear God, why?" I sobbed.

Papa allowed me to sob for a few minutes and then took my shoulders. "Your sisters need you now more than ever."

I held Lydia into the early hours of the morning as she sobbed and stroked Thaddeus's head that lay in my lap. He did not scream or sob, but the wetness of my tunic was proof of his silent tears and broken heart. Mama comforted Anna, while Miriam held on to Abigail. When Andrew and I left, we stopped at Mary and Joseph's home to check on their family, but they were not there. The house was quiet, empty of all belongings, and the gifts from the Magi were vacant from the shelf.

Three weeks later, I gave birth to a beautiful baby boy whom Andrew and I named Samuel. The next year passed by with gentle ease as I navigated being a new mother. Although there would always be pieces missing from their hearts that their sons once filled, my sisters slowly began engaging in life again. I worried the birth of my son would cause my sisters heartache, but his presence brought them joy. Each week, I would visit one of my sisters to check on them. If the events of the horrific night a year ago taught me anything, it was the importance of investing in those you love, because life can change in an instant.

CHAPTER 20

I walked up the hill—the cabin was in sight. The day was cooler than usual, but the sun shined bright. I looked beside me. No longer did Haste walk behind me with his heartbreaking limp. He trotted beside me with beautiful agility, looking like a newborn lamb fresh with life. "Are you enjoying this walk, Haste?" My beloved lamb bleated in joy, soaking up the brisk air and beautiful surroundings.

A soft little hand touched my cheek, filling my heart with more exquisite joy, I thought it might burst. "Ma-Ma." I adjusted the wrap that held my son and smiled down at baby Samuel. "Mama's sweet angel. Guess who you get to see today. Your aunt and cousins. What a joyous time that will be." Samuel's face lit up with a smile. I could say anything really, and my child would smile. At this phase in his life, I was his whole world. "Here we are."

Knock, knock, knock. "Come in!" I heard a voice say on the other side of the door.

Slipping my shoes off, I opened the door. "Hello, Sister! I hope you are available for some company."

Miriam looked up from the bread she was kneading. "Of course! Come in, please."

Samuel, Haste, and I walked into the tiny cabin. Miriam wiped her hand on a towel. Dropping the towel on the table, she walked over and embraced me. "You know you are always welcome here. Now, hand over my nephew."

I rolled my eyes. "I see how it is now. I come second. Everyone wants to see the baby."

Miriam took Samuel from my wrap. She held him close and kissed him on the cheek. "You better get used to that little sister." Miriam laughed. "Very soon, you will not have the room to carry him in that wrap."

I put my hands on my stomach. "Am I beginning to show?"

"A little bit, but it is not that noticeable. How's your sickness?"

"Much better. I feel as though it was not as bad with this baby."

"Well, thank God for that blessing. Savor it because it will be different with every child you carry." Miriam smiled as she said those words, but I could see the sadness in her eyes. Losing her son the way she did had aged her. Wrinkles that were not present a year ago curled around her eyes. And as a woman in her late twenties, she was far too young to have gray hair, but there they were, contrasted with her black hair. I shuddered in pain for my dear sister when I thought of what her heart might look like.

Whoosh! I looked over to see Thaddeus had thrown open the curtain leading to his room. "Aunt 'Dassa! I thought I heard you. Did you bring Samuel?

"Hmmm, no, I decided he was old enough to stay at home by himself."

As if in on my private joke, Samuel giggled in delight seeing his older cousin. Thaddeus crossed his eyes at me. "I knew you weren't telling the truth."

I shrugged my shoulders. "You are just too smart, Nephew. Here is a better question. Why are you not with your flock, young man?"

Thaddeus rolled his eyes. “Because Mama worries too much.”

I looked at my sister for the whole story. Miriam pointed at her son. “First, do not be so insolent and lower your voice because if you wake up your sisters after they just fell asleep, there will be no evening meal for you tonight.” She turned her attention to me. “Thaddeus has a cough, and there is a chill in the air. I did not want him to get any sicker.”

I opened my mouth to speak, but my nephew was quicker. “But Mama, ever since Asher died, you do not let me out of your sight. And when you do, it is only with Papa. I am eight years old, not a baby. This is the third time this month you have made me stay home from my flock!”

My sister took a step back. Her wide eyes and opened mouth made her look like she just had been slapped. I looked from my sister to my nephew, unsure of who to address first. My answer came when Samuel began crying, and I felt my milk rush to the surface. I walked over to my sister. “Here, give Samuel to me.” Miriam passed my screaming child to me and turned to the kitchen table. She gripped the edges of the cedar wood and dropped her head. “He is right.” My sister whispered through sobs. I rubbed my sister’s back in comfort. “Miriam, be kind to yourself. You went through the most horrible experience a mother could witness last year. Time will help. And it already has. You are not in bed all day anymore. You are functioning for your family again.”

“But I do not want to shelter my children. I want them to live life without fear.”

“You will get there, Sister. I promise.”

Miriam took a deep breath and wiped her tears.

“Go for a walk.”

My sister looked at me, bewilderment etched on her face. "What?"

"Go for a walk. I have to feed Samuel, so I will stay with the children while you take some time for yourself."

Miriam gave me a half smile. "I think I will. Thank you, Hadassah."

After Miriam left, I looked at Thaddeus. "Please, go get me a blanket, I need to feed your cousin."

Thaddeus left and emerged with a large wool blanket. I wrapped the blanket around my shoulder and positioned Samuel so he could eat. Quickly his whimpering ceased as he drank. Settling down on a pillow, I patted the pillow next to me. "Sit beside me, Thaddeus."

Thaddeus fell dramatically on the pillow as Haste took the opportunity to lay his head on my lap. I gave his head a good scratch and then looked at Thaddeus. "Are you okay?"

Thaddeus sighed. He shook his head in frustration. "I do not understand Mama. I miss Asher all the time, and I am so sad he died. But I still want to do everything I like—playing with my sisters, cousins, and friends, taking care of my flock. Does that make me wicked, Aunt Hadassah?"

I opened my free arm, inviting my nephew into my embrace. He cuddled up to my side and laid his head on my shoulder. "No, Thaddeus. That does not make you wicked. You are not going to grieve like your Mama. You cried for many weeks after your brother died, and that is what your heart needed. But you must understand this. A mother's love for her children is special, a connection that is ... ethereal.

"What is ethereal?"

"It means refined, unworldly. It is what she feels for you and each one of your sisters. The loss of one of her children feels like she lost a part of herself. So, what you must understand is you are not going to understand your mother's grief. The best gift you can give her is grace. Okay?"

Thaddeus's eyes were large and solemn. "Okay," he whispered.

"Now," I said, hoping to change the sinister mood, "how about I tell you a story?" I loved the tradition of telling the stories of our lives to our children so they can remember, tell their children as they grow and have families of their own. Eventually, entire generations of Jewish people knew our story, and that is how a person's legacy lives on even when they are gone.

"Yes! Tell me about the story of how you met Jesus."

I chuckled. "I just told you that story, Thaddeus."

"But it is my favorite."

I smiled. "Mine too. Well, this story starts out sad. It was my last day to be with my flock because the next year I would remain home with your grandmother to learn the final lessons I needed to become a wife and run a home, honoring our Jewish heritage. The next day, I would become betrothed—

"To Uncle Andrew!"

"Yes, to Uncle Andrew. But I was devastated. I loved my mama, but I did not want to run a Jewish home, I wanted to run my flock. But after a lot of prayer, I was no longer angry and bitter. I understood why it was important for a Jewish woman to be married, so I accepted what was expected of me."

"Why is it important for a Jewish woman to be married?"

"That is for another story ... when you are much older. Anyway, because giving up being the family shepherd was so hard for me, I asked Papa if we could sleep with the flock that night—

"And you had never done that before.

I looked down at my nephew. "Yes, and you know this, Thaddeus, because I have told you this story about twenty times. The last time was just two weeks ago. Now, if you keep interrupting me, I will not finish this story until your nineth birthday." I said, my voice dryer than the desert sand. Thaddeus put his hand over his mouth, and I took that opportunity to bounce Samuel who had fallen asleep. When his little lips began moving, I knew he was eating again.

"Now, your grandfather was quick to agree, and after the evening meal, Papa and I headed to the sheep pasture." I smiled down at Haste who was sound asleep on my lap. "The night was perfect. The stars lit up the sky, and I sat surrounded by my sheep. I think they sensed a change was coming because they would not leave my side. I made sure I had a special time with each sheep to tell them goodbye and how much they meant to me. Eventually, it was time to go to bed."

"The best part is next!" He gasped and threw his hand over his mouth.

I grinned. "It is okay, I will forgive you because you are right, this *is* the best part. As I was laying out our bedrolls, the sky split open and a beautiful angelic being appeared. It looked as if he was standing in the sky, his glow illuminating the night! We were terrified. But he soothed our fears. 'Fear not!' he bellowed. 'I bring you good tidings of great joy which shall be to all people. For unto you is born this day in the city of David, a Savior, which is Christ the Lord. And this shall be a sign unto you; ye shall find the babe wrapped in swaddling clothes, lying in a manger.' Then suddenly thousands of other angelic beings joined the first angel, and they began singing. It was the most beautiful singing I had ever heard. 'Glory to God in the highest,' they sang, 'and on earth peace, goodwill toward men.'"

"Amazing!"

"It was amazing! Papa was so sure the angels told us about Jesus and how to find him, because we were supposed to go to him. So, we gathered all the sheep and put them into the pen, even Haste. We started to walk away, and then the strangest thing happened. Haste started bleating and pawing at the gate. I always knew Haste had a special purpose, and in that moment, I knew it had something to do with Jesus. I quickly picked him up from the pen, and off we went to find the Messiah."

"So, you came with Haste," Thaddeus pointed at Haste and giggled.

I laughed and looked down at Haste who was awake now. "I suppose we did. When we finally made it to the city, we had to figure out where Jesus might be. We knew that if he was in a manger, he would not be in an inn. And then as if God whispered it in my soul, I knew."

"Great-grandfather's stable cave!"

"Exactly right! Oh, Thaddeus, when we came upon the baby with his mother, Mary, and his father, Joseph, it was the most beautiful sight. Mary and Joseph invited us in the cave to meet Jesus, and Mary asked if I wanted to hold him. I could not believe I was holding the Savior of the world. I was so mesmerized when the baby began crying. It is absurd to think about now, but I did not think the Christ child would cry. I tried to soothe him, but he would not stop his whimpering. I almost gave him back to Mary, but then out of the corner of my eye, I saw Haste limping toward me. When he was finally next to Jesus, Haste began nuzzling the baby to comfort him. Jesus's tears instantly ceased, and his little hand slipped out of his swaddling clothes to caress Haste's head. Then I watched in amazement as Haste's maimed hind leg slowly straightened into a perfect and whole limb."

"It was in that moment I knew Haste had fulfilled his purpose. And Papa did too, with the evidence of tears streaming down his face." I lifted the blanket off my sleeping son and laid him on the pillow beside me. I picked up Haste and cuddled him. "A maimed lamb that should have never lived, that could have defiled and disgraced our household if he died, a maimed male lamb that could never atone for Israel's sin—an outcast, an animal that people did not understand why he was alive, *he* was the one Yahweh chose to comfort his son, his chosen one. If that's not a divine purpose ..."

Thaddeus coughed. "Oh, Thaddeus, that cough sounds horrible. I would have made you stay in as well."

Thaddeus crossed his eyes at me and then asked a question I am sure he had been pondering for a long time. "What do you think *his* purpose is?"

I looked at him in confusion. I had just told him what Haste's purpose was. "Who are you talking about?"

"Jesus."

"Oh, I do not know. I am not sure how he will fulfill his role as the Messiah. No one knows." I tilted my head to the side as the thought occurred to me. "Well, maybe everyone except Haste." I looked down at my beloved companion and held him tighter. "Because when I think of my sweet, maimed lamb, my mind immediately goes to the night Haste, a lamb who could never atone for Israel's sin, comforted the Savior who came to this earth to atone for Israel. I believe that precious maimed lamb knew what all of us did not."

I smiled down at my nephew. "Haste showed me and so many others that God has a purpose for everyone. Even when a person, or yes, even a lamb, seems insignificant to the world, God sees their significance. Haste proves that.

Every morning, I sit in my favorite chair by the window, feeding Samuel, and as always, Haste is lying right by my feet. I remember the angel announcing Jesus's birth, and whenever the gentle wind blows through the flowers and the trees, I know I hear angelic choirs singing, "Glory to God in the Highest and on earth peace, goodwill toward men."

Shalom, Dear Reader! Thank you so much for reading *And They Came with Haste*. If there are some words you aren't sure of the meaning, I have included a word glossary to help you understand some of the Jewish traditions and Hebrew words. Once again, whether you have been one of my readers or this is the first time you have picked up one of my books, I want you to know I appreciate you!

ABOUT THE AUTHOR

In 2013, Whitney was diagnosed with a rare genetic mutation. In fact, so rare that she was the first person to have ever been diagnosed with the disease, and the mutation so rare and horrific that she should not have survived her mother's pregnancy. After years of research on the disease, Whitney was invited to give the new phenomena a name. She chose to name it *MAGIS Syndrome*. MAGIS is the Latin word for more. She hoped the meaning would give future patients who are diagnosed with MAGIS Syndrome the assurance that they are MORE than their disease. Whitney hopes through her story, people of all ages will know, despite the mountains they face, they are MORE!

GLOSSARY OF WORDS:

El Chuwl: Name of God meaning "the God who gave you life."

Elohim: The name of God meaning strength and might.

Gambol/Gamboled: Rub or jump around playfully. Sheep often gamboled at the sight of their shepherd. Their shepherd was their whole world. This was the person who cared for them and kept them safe from predators and any other dangers.

Gentiles: Gentiles are anyone who is not of the Jewish race.

Hallel Psalms: The Psalms of Praise.

Jehovah Jireh: One of the many names of God. This name means "The LORD will provide." It is the name Abraham declared when God provided the ram in place of his son Isaac to be sacrificed.

Lambing Process: Physical signs the ewe experiences that signals she is in beginning labor.

Mantle: 1) Loose sleeveless cloak or shawl. 2) Important role or responsibility that passes from one person to another.

Passover: A Jewish holiday celebrating God's promise of freeing the Jews from the bond of the Egyptians and to remember the twelve plagues God used to convince Pharaoh to release God's people.

Prophecy: A prediction about the future that a person or a body of people is supposed to fulfill.

Purification for a Woman: In the Jewish culture, every woman was required to purify herself after her menstrual cycle.

Receptacle: A small bag for holding objects. Shepherds carried slings and stones to defend their sheep from predators, ointment for the sheep's sores, and shepherds like Hadassah who could play an instrument, kept their small instrument in this small pouch.

Yahweh: Another name of God. Yahweh actually comes from the Hebrew word, "I am."

Sacrificial Lamb: Every household was to bring an animal to Jerusalem to sacrifice. God had specific instructions on what animals were suitable for sacrifice, based on the financial station of the household.

Simlah: The outer form of Jewish men and women's clothing. Typically, heavy and thick.

Tahoo: This was what the shepherd called out when they needed their sheep to assemble. When the sheep heard this word, they knew they were to gather at their master's side.

Tetelistai: Hebrew word meaning complete or "it is finished." Shepherds proclaimed this word when one of the sheep died, signaling their time with the flock had ended.

The Torah: The first five books of the Bible: Genesis, Exodus, Leviticus, Numbers, and Deuteronomy. Also known as the Pentateuch and the Books of Moses—the author of the books and leader who led the Israelites out of Egypt.

Unclean: Immoral or dietary acts or immorality. This could be something a Jew consumed like pork or touched such as a dead animal or if they performed a lewd or sexual discretion.

Unleavened Bread: Bread without yeast. The Jews were instructed to eat unleavened bread during Passover because leavened bread was a metaphor for sin in the Bible.

Yahweh-Yireh: The name of God meaning, "the LORD will provide."

CHARACTER DISCUSSION QUESTIONS

Hadassah:

1) Change and the idea of the unknown frightened Hadassah. Overcoming the panic was a process for Hadassah, but she finally learned to trust in her God, because he never changed or forgot his promises. How do you work through your fear? Think of all the promises he has kept for you.

2) Do you agree with Hadassah's belief that it's okay to try to understand God's ways instead of just simply accepting them? Do you think that kind of thinking is rebellious, even though Hadassah would never turn her back on God's ways? Have you ever questioned God or asked him why he chose to do what he did?

3) Despite Hadassah's flaws, she has compassion, a servant's heart, and is sensitive to God's leading. Hadassah knew God was compelling her to fight for Haste, but he didn't put that understanding to spare the lamb in any of the other shepherds. Why do you think God puts certain callings and messages on a one person's heart but doesn't place that message on other hearts?

Samuel:

1) Samuel is an earthly picture of how our Heavenly Father sees his children. What are some godly traits you saw in Samuel as you were reading?
2) In contrast, we also saw Samuel's humanity as he admitted to Hadassah what he struggled with. Are you able to admit what you struggle with like Samuel did?
3) Samuel feels his territory of providing for his daughter has been threatened due to Andrew walking Hadassah to and from the sheep pasture. Pride and jealousy are sides of Samuel we had never seen before. Have you ever acted out of character so much that you hurt other people? How did you handle the aftermath?

Rachel:

1) In some ways, Rachel is more traditional and legalistic than her husband, Samuel. Do you think it's because of the pressure women had in those days of making their husband look honorable by keeping her household up to the standards of Jewish society?
2) Rachel even acted out of character in the story when she slapped Hadassah. It was out of fear of what others would think. This same fear is still present today, probably even more so. How do you overcome the fear of what others think of you?
3) It is so evident that Samuel and Rachel have a special kind of love and bond. How do you think they created this bond living in a period of time where women were viewed as nothing more than property and child bearers?

Lydia:

1) Lydia is such a loving confidant to Hadassah. These two women are more than sisters, they are best friends. What traits do you see in her that make her a good encourager? How can you apply that to your life?
2) Lydia's trust in Samuel is a picture of how we should trust God. Lydia had no fear of marriage because she trusted Samuel and knew he'd arrange a betrothal of tenderness and not gruffness. How do you trust God in different situations?
3) Lydia's reminder to Hadassah to take one day at a time and enjoy the season she was in is good wisdom for us all. What you can you do to make the season you are in count?

Andrew:

1) Andrew could have resigned from being a hireling to pursue his carpentry business, but stayed because he loved Hadassah, and he wanted to get to know the woman God created her to be. How can you invest in those that you love as Andrew invested in Hadassah?
2) Andrew was put in a very awkward situation when he was reprimanded by Samuel because he walked with Hadassah to ensure she made it to the sheep pasture and returned home safely. Andrew responded with respect despite his superior being in the wrong. Have you ever had to take the high road when someone criticized you or told you you were wrong when you weren't? How did that make you feel?
3) On Hadassah and Andrew's wedding night, Andrew comforted a terrified Hadassah by telling her the night would go their way, and they would not do

anything until she was ready. In a time where consent wasn't heard of and a husband being harsh with his wife was accepted, Andrew emulated how God intended sex to be—tender. What traits are you looking for in a spouse? Are they God-centered?

Haste:

1) Why do you think God used a maimed lamb to comfort Jesus and foreshadow what the baby's purpose was on this earth?

Made in United States
North Haven, CT
12 January 2023

30993521R00089